The Skinkadink

Bradler Smith

Bradler Smith

*For my partner Kerry
and my two little boys, Bradley and Tyler*

Contents

Prologue

Wilstrome was a vast and beautiful ancient woodland realm, which, as well as dense woods, was made up of many curious and mysterious landscapes. Peculiar wildflower meadows in every colour imaginable, from tiny flowers the size of microscopic insects to predatory man-eaters that soar into the sky. Mushroom forests which towered as high as the tallest, mightiest oak and everything in between. Breathtaking but perilous rivers thunder through the trees and meadows and over cliffs set into the woodland hills creating spectacular waterfalls. The entire realm is surrounded by mountains, home to mysterious caves and equally baffling creatures, which stalk and lurk deep into the barren landscape surrounding Wilstrome. This made exit and entry somewhat difficult, few ever left and even fewer made it safely into Wilstrome. The inhabitants of the woodlands consisted of many species, humans, dwarves, magical and mystical, creatures tiny, gigantic and the unknown. They have all made their home in Wilstrome. You name it, it was here exploring, prowling or lurking somewhere in the woods.

It's deep in these woods where you could find the village of Walnut Point. The village got its name from the many towering, thick walnut trees which act as dwellings for the residents of the village. Houses had been cut into the large trees over the years creating the homes and shops that make up the little village. One of these walnut trees was home to two good friends, Plodweasel and Tamfoot.

Plodweasel was a weasel, of normal weasel-like proportions, except with an increased level of grumpiness, which arose in any given situation. His fur was short and brown, with white fur covering his belly, running from his neck to his hind legs. He could always be seen carrying a little crooked walnut cane, in a leather sword belt, attached to his back. He generally used the cane for pointing at other woodland creatures and thudding it on the floor, when going through regrettably frequent bursts of grumpiness. In past adventures, he also used the cane for fighting. The end of the walnut cane, about a third of its length, could be removed like a sheath to reveal an impossibly sharp blade. Although a seemingly grumpy fellow, Plodweasel was of good heart and would do anything for his best friend Tamfoot and for that matter, any of the residents of Walnut Point.

Plod's best friend, Tamfoot, was an extremely rare, seldom seen species known as a two-footed scritch, as opposed to the now extinct three footed variety. About the size of a domestic cat, he stood on two webbed feet, slightly hunched over with short fur covering his entire body, apart from his wings and feet. He had black and yellow banding around the body much like a bumble bee and had little claw-like hands protruding from white, near translucent wings. The two-footed scritch are naturally very happy, good-natured creatures, if somewhat over excitable at times and could be quick to make poor judgments; this is what unfortunately led to the eventual downfall of the larger three footed variety of scritch. He had a yellow, oval-shaped head with large light-blue eyes and short furry ears. No one actually knew how to make the distinction between a male and female two-footed scritch or how to determine its age, this included Tamfoot himself. For clarification, Tamfoot is referred to as "he" in this tale. The origins of the two-footed scritch are also a mystery, or at least a mystery to the few who are even aware the species existed and have had the pleasure to meet such an intriguing and extraordinary creature.

Plod's general grumpiness is thought to come from the fact that he had spent too much time brooding over his last adventure, which occurred a few years previously, but did not come to a successful conclusion. At the time he was the most successful adventurer in the village of Walnut Point. The village elder, the dwarf, Frilldar the Great (no one was quite sure what "the great" was exactly in honour of, other than his exceptional old age) had tasked Plod with joining other worthy adventurers from villages and towns across Wilstrome, to protect it from an almighty and awful foe, a Skinkadink.

The Skinkadink is an ancient creature that dwelled somewhere within the cavernous mountains that surround Wilstrome. It frequently made its way down into the woods to prey on the creatures of the woodlands. It was thought that food was scarce within the mountain ranges and this would give the Skinkadink reason to descend and feast on the inhabitants of the wood, terrorising villages and towns and leaving destruction and despair in its wake. The foul creature was a gigantic bird that stood as tall as a large oak on lean but short, powerful legs. It could only just about fly due to its massive bulk but was able to glide quite majestically. Its enormous beak curved downwards to a razor-sharp point and was filled with hundreds of backwards-facing teeth, each five inches long. It's entire dark grey body and head had a hard bone-like appearance, except its wings, which were covered in ragged scars and tears from many battles over the years. Its eyes were like shiny, piercing black gemstones, which gave the beast a sinister, malevolent stare. The fearsome predator was also armed with large, hooked claws on its wings and feet, which had served it well over the hundreds of years that it had terrorised Wilstrome. No one knew exactly how long the Skink-adink had hunted and preyed on the folk of the woods, the one thing they did know was; they never knew a time without the looming threat of this hideous beast.

A few years ago, Plod and his brave band of adventurers were tasked with finding and defeating the Skink-adink once and for all. Ultimately, Plod was the only one to survive, having courageously fought the monster alongside his companions. They failed to defeat it and his comrades perished in the battle. He fled the mountains, but being badly injured, he passed out on the outskirts of Wilstrome where he was discovered by an unusual creature, a two-footed scritch that went by the name of Tamfoot. The scritch are a magic species and Tam used his healing energy to save Plod. Once recovered, the weasel asked the creature to join him on his return to the relative safety of Walnut Point. They became great friends and although, like most two-footed scritch, Tam had no permanent place to call his home due to endlessly exploring the woods, he decided to take up residence with his new friend. They had lived happily in Plod's Walnut tree house for the past few years, regardless of his intermittent mood swings and grumpiness.

No one had heard of attacks from the Skinkadink over these last few years and some thought, maybe the quest was successful, and the beast had succumbed to its wounds from the battle or had perished from old age. But this was soon about to change ...

Chapter 1

'Plod!' Tam called out in his soft, friendly voice. 'A letter has arrived for you, it has "urgent" written on it.' Tam picked up the folded letter, which had been slid under their walnut door at first light and he flew up to Plodweasel, who was still asleep in their bedroom. Tam's wings didn't flutter aggressively at great speed like a fly, they had much slower, majestic flap. Their house, like all the dwellings in Walnut Point, were carved skilfully into the magnificent walnut trees by master carpenters that had lived for many generations in the village. They were a dwarven species, whom worked their entire lives with wood and their reputation as carpenters was unrivalled throughout all of Wilstrome. Plod and Tam's house consisted of four rooms, which rose up through the trunk of the tree. The houses were laid out, to make the best use of the available space. A spiral staircase made entirely out of walnut, twisted up through all four floors and a couple of windows were positioned at opposite ends of each room. The first and largest floor contained an impressive fireplace carved into the wood, which was lined with iron. An ornate iron chimney jutted out the side of the tree at a crooked angle, and a wisp of smoke slowly snaked into the branches above. A thick, sturdy looking dining table and comfortable looking furniture was also laid out on the ground floor. Everything was expertly carved out of walnut, as were most things in Walnut Point. The second floor contained a kitchen with various pots and pans scattered about the place and the third floor was a bedroom, which had two comfy looking beds at opposite sides of the room, along with a couple of chairs and desks and a large wooden trunk at the foot of each bed. The trunk of the ancient tree tapered upwards and led into the fourth and final room, which was also the smallest. It contained an old telescope that was directed towards the sky and out of a little oval-shaped window. Two tankards plus a deck of cards lay on a table between two chairs.

'Tam, why do you insist on rising so early every morning? It's not like we have anything particularly important to be getting on with!' grumbled the weasel in his assertive, slightly gruff voice. 'What's this letter all about? We don't usually get letters, seems unusual to me,' mumbled Plod as he fell out of bed and proceeded to have a good stretch before slipping on his leather belt and attaching his sword cane. 'OK, Tam, let's see what's in this "urgent" letter.' Tam handed his friend the letter and he studied it carefully, his eyes narrowing as he seemed to take on a slightly more serious expression.

'Well Plod, anything important?' asked Tam, keen to know the contents.

'It's direct from the old dwarf himself,' replied Plod. 'Old Frilldar seems to be spooked about something or other. He actually mentions us both in the letter. He wants us to meet him in his tree for an urgent meeting as soon as we've had breakfast and says not to tell anyone else about this.'

'Hmm, sounds mysterious, I wonder what Frilldar needs help with?' said Tam, hovering around the room with a hint of nervous excitement in his voice.

'Well, I wouldn't get too excited Tam,' said Plod, 'The old dwarf's probably lost his coin pouch again and doesn't trust anyone else to help him find it. It wouldn't be the first time and I would bet all my coin that it won't be the last,' he remarked dismissively. 'Let's have something quick for breakfast and then we'll go help the foolish old dwarf.' The two friends descended the winding walnut staircase to the kitchen below and put on a pot of herbal tea and toasted some thick, crusty bread, slathering it in strome berry jam. This was a large, juicy, bright red berry the size of an apple, native to Wilstrome. Once they'd finished, they made their way over to dwarf Frilldar's tree, which was a five-minute walk to the other end of Walnut Point. A small brook meandered its way through the walnut trees and into the centre of the village to an old stone bridge, which arched over the fast-flowing brook.

Chapter 2

Tam carefully dropped down to the floor and they both walked up to Frilldar's front door. Plod stood up on his hind legs and gave three decisive knocks, before dropping back down and waiting for a response. A minute later, just as Plod started shaking his head and was about to knock again, the old dwarf opened the door and looked around.

'Who goes there!?' demanded the old dwarf in his wizened voice. Plod and Tam looked at each other and raised their eyebrows before staring back up at Frilldar. 'Aha! My apologies, friends, I didn't see you down there!' Frilldar always spoke in a deafening voice. He was hard of hearing and would often hold a large ear trumpet to his ear to make out what others were saying. He had a thick, red, wiry beard and stood just under 4ft tall. He still had strong, broad shoulders and wore an old, thick, green woollen shirt stretched over his barrel chest with a waist coat over the top, dark green trousers and a pair of dusty looking, sturdy strapped boots. Frilldar was extremely old, no one knew exactly how old, not least the old dwarf himself, and he was the leader of Walnut Point. Wilstrome was not governed by anyone in particular but most of the villages and towns throughout Wilstrome had a leadership figure of some sort. In times of great importance or in a crisis, prominent leaders would come together to help one another for the good of Wilstrome, this is how things had worked for hundreds of years. Frilldar ushered his friends inside quickly and gave one last look around in an uneasy manner, as if checking no one had seen them before quickly closing the door.

'So, Frilldar, why all the secrecy? I assume it's the whole lost coin pouch issue again, Hmm?' queried Plod.

'I just wish it were something so trivial, friends,' replied Frilldar. 'No this is regarding a far graver matter.' The old dwarf was sweating and starting to look a bit queasy.

'You're not looking so good,' said Tam. 'Why don't you take a seat and I'll fetch you a glass of water.' Plod now looked concerned for his old friend and ushered him over to a seat by the fireplace. Tam quickly flew up to the kitchen to fetch the water. Frilldar's tree was set out much like Plod and Tam's, although it was slightly bigger and also had a cellar, where he mostly kept bottles of wine and mead and large rounds of cheese. Tam glided to a stop in front of the fireplace and handed the dwarf a glass of water.

'OK, Frilldar, now you're alarming us,' said Plod as Tam nodded worriedly. 'Come on what's troubling you?'

'The Skinkadink,' replied Frilldar flatly whilst studying the fire. 'I have definite confirmation from other leaders that the beast is stirring again.'

Plod stared aimlessly out the window and narrowed his eyes; he didn't say anything for a couple of minutes and just let the silence hang in the air. 'I knew this day would come,' replied Plod. 'Most folk in Wilstrome have started to forget the threat from the beast, it's been three years after all. We didn't defeat it on that fateful day, yes we injured it, badly, confined it to the mountains whilst it recovered and regained confidence maybe, but we didn't kill it.' Plod dropped his gaze as his eyes seemed to well up, remembering his lost comrades. Tam and Frilldar wore sad expressions whilst they listened to their friend.

'I'm sorry Plod,' said Frilldar as he softly touched the weasel's paw with a callused hand. 'We should have taken your concerns more seriously my friend, we became too complacent. It's no wonder you have been so withdrawn these past few years.'

'No, you don't need to apologise,' replied Plod. 'What could we have done anyway? Folk wanted to forget and move on without thinking about the threat from the monster. Who could blame them, especially when month after month passed without any sight of the Skinkadink. Tell me about the confirmation you have from the other leaders, Frilldar.'

'I'm afraid it's troubling news,' began Frilldar with a catch in his voice. 'As well as confirmed sightings of the beast high up in the northern Loftpeak mountains, farm animals have also been disappearing late at night without a trace from villages on the outskirts of Wilstrome, which border the base of Loftpeak. All the leaders agree that the Skinkadink has been biding its time these last few years and regaining its strength. Lying in wait to attack, when the folk of Wilstrome have let their guard down and the lingering threat of the beast has started to slip from their minds.'

Tam looked from Frilldar to Plod open-mouthed whilst Plod shook his head, 'It's starting again,' said Plod. 'It won't be long before it's smashing through villages and towns again, leaving a devastating trail of death and destruction in its wake.'

'Yes, Plod, this is why we need to take quick and decisive action,' said Frilldar. 'The other leaders and I have all agreed, as you are the only creature alive today with experience of fighting the Skinkadink, we have no choice but to ask for your help. You are the sole surviving member of the last Skinkadink hunting party and thus, ask that you form a new band of adventures, Plod, and destroy this hideous creature before it obliterates our entire community.'

Plod stared back out the window and didn't say anything. After a long silence, Tam spoke, 'You can count on me, Plod. What choice do we have, you know we have to try otherwise the constant threat of the Skinkadink will return.' Frilldar nodded sagely towards Tam with a serious expression on his face. Plod lowered his gaze once more and simply left Frilldar's tree without saying a word. 'Don't worry, Frilldar, I'll speak to him, you know you can count on us.' The old dwarf nodded in Tam's direction without a hint of uncertainty on his face.

Tam headed back towards their tree and spotted Plod sitting on the stone wall of the bridge, over the brook in the centre of the village. He was staring into the water and looked lost in his thoughts. Tam approached his friend and sat on the wall next to him. 'It's been a long time since my adventuring days, Tam,' remarked Plod after a couple of minutes. 'I'm out of practice with my sword cane and currently it's just me and you in the party. I haven't seen anyone from my adventuring days for the last few years and wouldn't know where to start,' he said hopelessly.

'No, I'm sorry Plod, but I won't let you slip into one

of your moody, depressive states. Today I'm going to help you put some practice in with your sword cane and then I'll tell you where we're headed first. I know a creature not too far from here, whom I think would be a worthy addition to our party, she has aided me in the past.'

'Really? Who is she?' queried Plod.

'First the training then the explaining,' replied Tam with a big grin.

Plod looked at his friend and smirked, trying not to laugh, 'OK then, Tam, let's get this show on the road.'

Tam was gifted with magic, primarily healing magic and was not much of a fighter, but he was happy to help his friend practice. He was eager to see what his friend was capable of. He had heard stories of Plods exceptional talent in battle with his sword cane – which he kept impossibly sharp – but in all the time that Tam had known him, he had never witnessed his friend's prowess with his cane. Plod gave Tam a sack of strome Berries and asked him to fly high and launch a berry towards him as hard as he could, he would then attempt to slice through the berry before it smashed onto the ground. 'OK, Plod, are you ready?' said Tam with an excitable grin.

'Yep, give me your best shot,' replied Plod. He slid off the sheath on his cane and slotted it into a little loop on his leather belt. He stood on his hind legs and swooshed it around a few times from side to side at excessive speed and it made a low, unsettling, pulsing sound as it cut through the air.

'Here I go!' shouted Tam as he soared high into the

air with a few powerful flaps from his wings. He curved backwards whilst performing a dramatic spin and shot towards where Plod was stood. He had one of the strome berries already in his hand and launched it as hard as he could towards Plod, fully expecting his friend to miss the first attempt as he got his eye in. Plod sprinted and jumped whilst arching his back and somersaulted, seemingly in slow motion and with great skill, never taking his eye off the fruit, flying towards the ground at speed. He reached a height that seemed near impossible for a creature of Plod's small stature and swung his sword cane so fast, all that could be seen was a flash of light from the sun, glinting off the blade as the berry exploded in a cloud of red pulpy juice.

Plod landed on his hind legs without the slightest wobble, as he swung the sword from side to side with purpose and precision. With his face covered in the red juice - which didn't seem to bother the weasel at all - he licked some from his cheek with a crooked grin and shouted, 'Again!' Tam squealed in delight; he could scarcely believe his eyes as he spun back into the air to go again.

Frilldar leant against his tree, he smoked a pipe and watched Plod and Tam darting about at the other end of the village. He looked on with a smile as he watched the weasel strike every berry with expert precision and skill. Sometimes, Tam would throw more than one at a time and Plod never missed his mark. He laughed to himself and said, 'looks like we've got our weasel back.' He watched the two friends until the sun went down and then went back into his tree, pleased with what he had seen.

Dusk was drawing in as Plod and Tam felt weary from

a full day of flying, sprinting and jumping, as Plod practised his craft for the first time in at least three years. They agreed to have a quick meal that night and get an early night's sleep, they would visit Frilldar at first light and give him the good news; they would take up the quest.

Chapter 3

For the first time since the two friends had both lived together in Walnut Point, Plod was the first to rise and had a renewed spring in his step. He had proven the day before, his skill with the sword cane was still in him and it felt good to charge about yesterday slicing through the strome berries. Ultimately, though, he had fun with his best friend, and he felt like he had a renewed purpose in his life. Tam rose just before first light, as he always did and was happy to hear his friend pottering about in the kitchen. Tam hopped down the first few steps of the spiral walnut staircase and gently flew down the rest of the way to the kitchen below, with a single flap of his wings.

Plod smiled at Tam when he entered the kitchen, 'Good morning, Tam, I eh ... I apologise for my overly grumpy temperament these last few years ... I know I've been difficult at times,' remarked Plod as Tam sat at the kitchen table.

'Ha! No need to apologise,' Tam replied 'Everyone knows why you haven't been yourself and anyway, I love it here, you just needed to get your mojo back.' Tam wore a big grin as he tucked into the toasted crusty bread and berries Plod had prepared for him. Plod chuckled at his friend and brought a pot of herbal tea over to the table and sat down.

'Once we've finished our breakfast, Tam, let's make our way over to the old dwarf and give him the good news: we will take up the quest. We should also find out exactly how he wants us to proceed on this quest, it's not going to be easy, I for one should know ...' Tam nodded in agreement at these words as he finished his breakfast.

After finishing breakfast, they left their tree and headed over to Frilldar. There wasn't a cloud in the sky and the strong morning sun created a light fog as water evaporated off the village brook. He was already outside, smoking his pipe and smiled when he saw them approach. 'Ahh, the great adventurers return,' Frilldar said with a smile whilst blowing a large ring of smoke into the air. 'I trust you have good news for me, friends? Going on your practice yesterday, Plod, I would say, you're looking very impressive. In fact, you both put on a remarkable display. I didn't realise you had such skill in the air, Tam, very good, very good indeed.' Frilldar puffed another large smoke ring into the air.

Tam and plod grinned at each other as Tam let out a little chuckle and curtsied to the dwarf. 'Thank you Frilldar,' said Tam, pleased with himself.

'Right, come on in you too, we have important business to discuss,' replied Frilldar. They sat by the fire in Frilldar's ground floor room. 'I take it, Plod, you are willing to accept this momentous quest?'

'Yes, as Tam said yesterday, I can't just sit around and

do nothing whilst that detestable beast gains strength and confidence by the day. We are both ready and willing to take up the quest,' confirmed Plod.

'Excellent news,' said the dwarf. 'I knew you still had it in you, Plod and the addition of Tam here is more than welcome. Your prowess in the air and the healing magic of the two-footed scritch will be an excellent addition to the party.

'How would you like us to proceed?' asked Tam. 'Do you have any other information at hand that can aid us on our quest?'

'I'm afraid it's like I said the other day,' replied Frilldar 'We need to stop the Skinkadink before it terrorises the folk of Wilstrome again. You will need to form a band with whom you think are able enough to defeat the monster. This will all be down to you, friends. The one thing I will add is, speed and stealth will be the key. I would recommend a small and able party, travelling light and fast. Time is of the essence, are you able to prepare to leave by this afternoon?

'No ... we'll leave this morning, within an hour,' replied Plod. Tam nodded in agreement.

'Excellent, I have great faith in both of you,' said Frilldar with a serious expression. 'I look forward to congratulating you and your party when you return victorious from a successful quest, Godspeed, friends.' With that, Plod and Tam said their goodbyes to the old dwarf and went back to their tree for one last time before leaving.

'OK, Tam, we need to get our packs and make sure we have basic provisions and water,' said Plod. 'As Frilldar said, we should pack light. We'll leave bed rolls, tents and anything else that we don't need. We'll just have to make do and sleep under the stars.'

'Agreed,' replied Tam. 'I'll fetch our packs; you get the food and water together.' Plod nodded and ran up the walnut staircase to the kitchen and gathered some provisions. Tam flew up to the bedroom and took their packs from the trunks at the foot of their beds. The packs were both made from light brown leather. Plod's pack had pockets on either side and was well balanced when strapped to his back. Tam's was more of a conventional rucksack as he walked and flew in a more upright manner. Plod and Tam quickly gathered what they required and made their way to the front of their walnut tree. They both secured their packs and shared the provisions equally between them. Plod also had his leather sword belt, containing his sword cane, which he strapped to his back and shoulders. This meant he didn't have to worry about it dragging along the ground.

'Right then, Tam, this is it,' said Plod. His voice trailing off as he and Tam looked up at their beautiful walnut tree home, possibly for the last time. They stood for a minute in silence and gazed over the charming village of Walnut Point. They could make out the old dwarf, Frilldar, at the other end of the village, leaning against his tree as he smoked his pipe, watching them. He held up his pipe and nodded in their direction. They returned the gesture, and departed into the woods, for their quest had just begun.

Chapter 4

The two companions made their way through the dense woodland along overgrown paths, until the paths stopped, and their progress was slowed by a tangled web of branches and fallen logs. An army of crickets made ear-piercing, high-pitched sounds and the sun struggled to find its way through the canopy of huge leaves that hung off ancient, thick, distorted looking trees. It was only late morning, but light was dim as they travelled through this wood. 'So, Tam, where are you taking us?' asked Plod, intrigued as their progress slowed down to a gentle pace. 'You still haven't explained where we are going to locate our first party member?' Since they had made their way into the woods from Walnut point, Tam had taken the lead; as he had said the day before, he knew of a welcome addition to join their band.

'We head to Cresswood,' stated Tam.

Plod stopped in his tracks and looked to his friend, 'Cresswood? Are you sure, Tam?' replied Plod. 'We don't want to end up dead before we even get going, what about the big horns?' Cresswood was a most unusual place, it wasn't a wood of trees, but a wood of thick, gargantuan cress. Similar to what you would add to your sandwiches, except only … much, much bigger. Thick white stems, the circumference of a large oak, soar into the sky and colossal mint green leaves cast enormous shadows on the ground. This gives the woodland of cress a ghostly, shadowy appearance as the sun struggles to penetrate through the leaves. There are two main species of note in Cresswood, the small horn cress mites, which are small, friendly creatures around twice the size of Plod and their much larger counterparts, the big horn cress mites, which are immense, aggressive predators twice the size of an adult elk.

'Yes, we'll need to have our wits about us, Plod, but within Cresswood lies a place known as Cresswood Hamlet,' replied Tam with a smile. 'A little-known place, partly due to most folk and creatures avoiding Cresswood at all costs, but this place is home to many small horn cress mites. The big horns have always hunted the small horns, but the hamlet is relatively safe due to the high number of small horns that have taken up home there. They have burrows within the thick cress stems, which go deep underground. It's easy for them to burrow into the stems as they are relatively soft. The cress mite we are seeking is named, Ping. She once saved my life when I was travelling the outskirts of Cresswood. Usually, the big horns don't venture out so close to the perimeter of the wood, but this time I was unlucky. A big horn took me by surprise and tossed me into the air with its horn and was about to finish the job. I closed my eyes, dazed and too injured to fly. Once again, I was flung into the air, but something was different this time. I opened my eyes, to see a small horn. Ping hurled me onto her back, and we stormed through Cresswood with the enraged big horn charging after us in pursuit of its prey. Fortunately, we made it to the safety of the hamlet, where the other small horns emerged from their burrows and faced the big horn down. He let out an almighty roar that you could feel in the pit of your stomach and then stalked around the perimeter for a while, stomping his massive paws on the ground until he got bored and left us alone. Ping took me into her burrow and looked after me for a few days until I got my strength back and was able to fly out of Cresswood. We said we would meet again someday and I'm looking forward to seeing her, although I'm not sure she will be as thrilled, under the circumstances of our visit ...'

'Hmm, that's quite a story, Tam,' replied Plod. 'She does sound like a formidable creature; I just hope we find Ping and get out of Cresswood unscathed.' Plod had a concerned expression, fully aware of the dangers that lurk in the place they were headed. They continued onwards until they came across the unmistakable stems of the giant cress, which were dotted about between the now sparse woodland of trees, as they gave way for the thick stems of the cress. They cautiously walked amongst the giant cress as the sun shone down on them, through the scarce trees. It soon turned back to shade as the cress became more abundant, there were only a few yards between each towering stem. It felt quite imposing as the two companions quietly stalked their way deeper into Cresswood. They were on constant alert, as a prowling big horn could suddenly appear around one of the thick stems, in the gloom, at any moment.

The sun was starting to set and the shadows between the cress turned to a blanket of unearthly darkness. 'Tam,' said Plod. 'I don't think we can continue tonight. We can't risk tripping over and encountering a big horn in the dark. What can we do about shelter? The temperature will drop soon as well.' The weasel rubbed his sides and scoured the area, trying to work out what they could use for shelter, as they were both starting to feel the chill. 'Don't threat, Plod, I have an idea,' replied Tam. Plod looked at him blankly. 'The stems, Plod, the cress stems,' said Tam looking pleased with himself. Plod raised his eyebrows at his friend and grinned.

'Right you are, Tam, the stems. I'll use my sword cane, help me clear away the stem and we'll have a small burrow in no time,' stated Plod. The two friends removed their packs and quickly set about cutting away and removing the rubbery chunks of stem, until they had a burrow big enough for both of them and their provisions.

'I'm going to make use of some of the stem we've removed, Plod,' said Tam as he took a couple of flints from his pack as Plod looked on, slightly confused. He set about making a neat, small mound of stem chunks and cracked his flints together making a spark, which let out bright flashes in the nearly pitch-black burrow. Tam expertly got the fire going on the third spark and blew the stem until little embers began to shimmer and small flames raged until the stem was sufficiently alight.

'Ha! Good thinking, Tam,' said Plod, impressed with Tam's work. 'I'm glad you've got experience amongst the cress, Tam, obviously not the part where you were violently attacked and chased by a predatory big horn, but it's coming in handy all the same.' They both chuckled as Tam gave an appreciative bow.

'Can I borrow your sword cane for a second, Plod?' asked Tam as he threw a larger chunk of stem on the fire but kept it under control so as not to attract the unwanted attention of a curious big horn.

'Eh, yeah sure,' replied Plod. He handed the cane over

to his friend and watched with curiosity.

'You know, Plod,' started Tam as he took the sheath off the sword cane. 'The cress stems aren't just good as shelter and firewood, its actually pretty tasty. It has a strong peppery flavour, especially when roasted quickly on a fire, why don't you try some?'

Plod raised his eyebrows and watched on, 'Hmm, well I'll wait and see what you think first, Tam.'

Tam jabbed the blade into a lump of cress and slowly twirled the cress around, a few inches above the flame and for no more than half a minute. He then took the cress off the flame and inspected it briefly before biting into it. 'Very tasty, very tasty indeed, here try some, Plod, it tastes just like roasted red pepper.'

Plod was unsure but trusted his friend's judgement, he took the cane from Tam and took a tentative bite out of the roasted lump of stem. 'Wow, there is no end to the uses of this stuff is there, Tam, how did you know it was so good to eat?' asked Plod, biting into the final lump of cress from the blade, then stabbing another and roasting it.

'Well, after my short time staying with Ping, I got to see how the small horns live in Cresswood. They made good use of the cress, and this included eating it,' replied Tam, he chuckled at his friend as he took another large bite of roasted cress. He took too much, and his cheeks puffed out as he chewed.

'Right you are, Tam,' mumbled Plod as he tried to finish his meal.

'I think we should get some rest now,' stated Tam. 'We want to try and get a decent night's sleep before continuing on to Cresswood Hamlet.' Plod nodded in agreement. Before settling down for the night, they roasted a couple more lumps of the stem and then in no time, both quickly fell asleep. The fire flickered, keeping them warm in their make-shift burrow as they slept.

As early morning dawned, Plod woke Tam as he shivered. Narrow beams of light shot down through the large cress leaves, piercing the ground and sending up little whisps of smoky fog in every direction. A few small embers still gave a faint, dying glow in last night's fire. Everything was covered in a thin film of moisture and rather than try to get the fire going again, the two companions grabbed a strome berry each from their packs and had a drink from their water flasks.

'OK, Plod, let's get our packs together and head onwards, to the hamlet,' said Tam. Plod agreed and they packed their bags. Plod also reattached his sword cane belt and secured it over his back.

They continued their journey through the wood of giant shadowy cress, staying on high alert, constantly watching and listening out for the appearance of an unwelcome big horn looking for an easy meal. After trekking through the cress all morning, Plod suddenly came to a halt, as he heard the sound of something darting about up ahead. 'Tam!' hissed Plod, holding out his paw to signal "stop" to his friend.

'They're up ahead, Plod, don't worry, that's the sound of small horns scampering about in Cresswood Hamlet,' reassured Tam with a smile. 'We've made it, unscathed, to the place the small horns call home.' Plod breathed a sigh of relief and raised his paw to his head, relieved he wouldn't have to put his practice with the sword cane into action so soon. 'Come on let's introduce ourselves, they're quite welcoming creatures.'

Tam flew ahead as Plod followed behind, unsure what

to expect. He had never had dealings with the small horn cress mites before, not many had. They were solitary creatures, keeping to their own species. The reason for this, in part, was due to the fact that not many risked venturing into Cresswood due to the threat from big horns. Also, the hamlet was deep into the wood and Plod had never even heard of its existence, until Tam explained that's where they were headed.

Tam and Plod stood in the middle of Cresswood Hamlet and watched with interest as the creatures shot about the place, seemingly all very busy. Many were scurrying about with little wicker style baskets strapped to their backs, filled with lumps of the cress stem. Clearly everything in the hamlet revolved around this versatile crop. After a couple of minutes watching the small horns frantically go about their daily business, one of them slowed down and studied the visitors, which caused her to lose her concentration and stumble, falling over in a heap in front of the two friends with lumps of stem rolling off in all directions. 'Ohhh, ahhh! Sorry I nearly hit you, so sorry ...' muttered the small horn as she picked herself up from the floor.

Tam and Plod quickly helped her to her feet. 'Ping!' screeched Tam with excitement.

'Tam!' shrieked Ping, shocked to see her old friend back in the isolated hamlet. They both embraced and Ping gave a friendly nod in the direction of Plod, 'Are you going to introduce me to your friend here, Tam?'

'Why, of course, this is my very good friend, Plodweasel, or Plod, for short,' replied Tam. Plod held out a paw, Ping eagerly shook his paw and wore a friendly, welcoming smile.

'Honoured to meet you Plod. If you could both just throw those lumps of stem back into my basket, we'll make our way over to my burrow and you can explain the reason for your surprise visit.' Plod and Tam cleared up the fallen cress stem and followed Ping over to her burrow. The hamlet consisted of hundreds of neat, doorless arches carved into the thick cress stems, with roomy burrows dug into the stems.

'Please come on in,' said Ping as she welcomed the visitors into her burrow. Ping stood about the same height as Plod, she had dark brown armour-plated skin, that nearly covered her entire head and body and had the appearance of hard-looking scales. It even covered her four paws. She had a small, stubby, short-haired tail and a single, sharp horn about 5 inches long, protruding straight forward from the crown of her head. Her eyes were bright green little ovals, and she had a mouth full of fearsome, razor-sharp little teeth, but somehow still had a warm, friendly smile. The big horns are almost identical to the small horns in appearance other than their tremendous size. They stand twice the height of the largest elk and have two extremely sharp and imposing horns. They are positioned one above the other with the top horn protruding by up to 3ft and the lower horn reaching no more than one foot in length. They are cumbersome and slow, compared to their smaller counterparts but they are ferocious beasts, unlike the friendly small horns.

'Now, Tam, why have you ventured all the way out to Cresswood Hamlet?' said Ping as they all entered the burrow. 'I hope you're not in any trouble, is everything OK?'

'Well, Ping, I wish I could say this was just a passing visit to see an old friend,' replied Tam. 'But we have an urgent matter to discuss with you. Is there anywhere we can go, so we will not be overheard?'

'Oh, yes, of course,' replied Ping, the smile slipping from her face as it made way for concern. 'Follow me down to the cellar, you should remember it well, Tam, you spent a few days in there as you recovered from your savage big horn attack.' Ping opened up a wicker hatch that was on the floor, this made way to steps cut into the earth, which descended into the cellar. Wicker was one of the few other materials in the hamlet, likely made from the large willow trees on the outskirts of the northern side of Cresswood. Small horns would occasionally venture to the outskirts, for supplies and materials other than cress stem. The main ground floor section of the burrow had a small willow table and chairs plus various wooden bowls and baskets strewn around. They all walked down the earth steps into the cellar. A willow-made bed stood in one corner, with a table and chairs opposite. One side of the cellar had stacks of cut cress stem, strome berries and jugs of water. In the middle of the room was a fire pit lined with rocks. A hole was directly above the fire and this went off at an angle up to the surface to act as a chimney. It came out just behind the large stem in an area that wouldn't trip up an unsuspecting small horn.

'Thank you, Ping,' started Tam when they were all stood in the cellar. 'Plod and I have been tasked with a quest of utmost importance. I now reside in the village of Walnut Point with Plod. The village leader, an old dwarf by the name of Frilldar, has given us some unsettling news regarding the monster in the mountains, the Skink-adink. It has started to stir again and is suspected of being responsible for missing farm animals from villages bordering the Loftpeak mountains.'

Tam and Plod took it in turns to fill Ping in on the developments regarding the Skinkadink. Tam also explained Plod's experience as a respected adventurer and the details around the ill-fated quest, for which he was the sole survivor, a few years ago.

'Wow, so you're the famed weasel that survived that impossible mission,' said Ping, impressed. 'We even heard about that out here in the hamlet. I'm very sorry for the suffering you experienced fighting the beast, Plod. It's understandable that you were reluctant to undertake quests these past few years, after a knockback like that.' Ping gave plod a heartfelt glance and gently put her paw on his shoulder. Plod lowered his gaze as he thought about that fateful day.

'Thank you, Ping,' replied Plod.

'What do you say, Ping?' asked Tam. 'Will you assist us on this quest? I know this is short notice and the chance of success is slim, but time is running out and we need to gather an able band of adventurers, to take on and defeat the beast.' Tam was unsure of her response and would fully understand if Ping declined, as this quest would put them all in great peril.

'Of course I will,' Ping quickly responded. Plod and tam shot each other stunned glances, expecting that Ping would at least question the wisdom in fighting the Skink-adink and would want to take some time to consider her answer.

'Wow, really, Ping? No hesitation at all? You do know what you're signing up for and that you might not make it?' asked Plod.

'You're doing this for the safety of Wilstrome and believe it or not, even though I don't get out of Cresswood often and have the constant threat of the big horns to contend with, I love this crazy place,' replied Ping. 'Also, I get the chance to escape the hamlet and seek adventure, count me in.'

'Haha! Fantastic news, Ping, welcome aboard!' shrieked Tam, he flew around the cellar in celebration, causing Plod and Ping to laugh at their excited companion.

'I think you should both spend the night in my burrow, and we'll head out at first light,' said Ping as Tam ended his victory lap of the cellar. 'There's no point leaving late in the afternoon just before it gets dark, I'll get the fire going and prepare a couple of make-shift beds.'

'Great, thank you, Ping,' replied Plod. 'That's settled then, we'll get a good night's sleep and head out first thing, you can guide us via the shortest route out of Cresswood'

'No problem,' replied Ping. 'I also have a suggestion of where we could head next.' Plod and Tam nodded, welcome to any suggestions of where they may be able to recruit new members to their party. 'The shortest route out of Cresswood is north towards the willow trees, the large river, the River Olden passes through the willows. You don't have to follow the river far west until you get to the small, human fishing village of Clamshell Nook.

With the route agreed by the new band of three, they roasted some lumps of cress on Ping's fire and then turned in for an early night, keen to set out in the morning for the fishing village, Clamshell Nook.

∞∞∞

Ping rose first, her adrenaline levels increasing, excited if somewhat wary to embark on this quest. She made a pot of hot cress and strome berry tea and her two companions awoke shortly afterwards to the sweet smell of the fragrant brew. 'That smells wonderful,' said Tam, rubbing his eyes. It was very early in the morning, just before first light; the sun still hadn't risen to a height where it could pierce the large canopy of monster cress leaves, high above the woodland floor. 'We should enjoy some of this tea and have something to eat, then set off as soon as possible, what do you think, Plod?'

'Excellent idea,' replied Plod, also rubbing his eyes. 'We have no time to waste, let's have our breakfast and get ready to leave, we don't want to be spending another night out in Cresswood away from the safety of the hamlet.'

They made quick work of the tea and breakfast and gathered their provisions together. Plod and Tam replenished their water flasks and restored their food supplies with strome berries and cress stem from Ping's cellar. Once finished, they strapped on their leather packs to their backs and Plod reattached his sword cane, securing it to the belt on his back. Ping used water to distinguish the fire in the cellar and got her own provisions ready. Her pack differed from her comrades, as it was made of willow wicker, as were many things in Cresswood Hamlet. The pack consisted of two willow baskets with lids, secured with leather cord, one on either side of her waist, which was fastened to her back with leather straps. She packed food and water, making sure the weight was evenly spread in both baskets.

The three companions stood outside Ping's burrow, packed and ready to leave by first light. 'OK, Ping,' said Plod. 'Would you like to say any goodbyes before we leave? I can't be certain … when you will return.'

Ping walked slowly into the centre of the hamlet and appeared slightly tearful as she took in her surroundings, possibly for the last time. It was too early for any of the other small horns to be awake and she didn't want to disturb them. She also feared they would try and warn her from going on the quest and attempt to change her decision. Her mind was set, and she wasn't about to spread fear unnecessarily throughout the hamlet with news of the Skinkadink. She trotted over to her two friends with a renewed spring in her step, excitement giving way to sadness and fear. Tam rested a claw-like hand on her shoulder and gave her a sincere look, 'Ready, Ping?'

'Follow me!' said Ping, trying not to raise her voice too loud and alerting the other small horns. Plod and Tam ran and flew after Ping as she shot into Cresswood, headed north to the willow trees on the outskirts of the wood.

They were making rapid progress as Ping's expert knowledge of Cresswood meant they were on course to reach the willow trees and the River Olden, which ran through them, by early afternoon. Unbeknownst to the brave band of adventurers, something had picked up their scent and was following their trail. A large, hungry, female big horn was keen for a meal to feed her young and now had them in her sights. She took a wide route around them and started to gallop, at speed, her aim was to head them off up ahead and take them by surprise.

'Not long now, guys!' shouted Ping, not turning around to her companions as she ran, nor did she have time to register the big horn charging towards her from her right. 'Were making excellent progress and will be at the willows in no time. Ahhhhrgh!' Ping let out a sickening shriek as the big horn suddenly came out of nowhere and tossed her into the air with her top horn. Ping bounced off a cress stem and slid across the ground, the lids on her wicker baskets flapped open and her provisions scattered in all directions.

'Ping!' screamed Plod. The big horn was headed straight for them now. Tam flew through the creature's legs with fly-like reactions, this caused the creature to fiercely shake its head, grunting, unsure of what had just happened as it headed straight for Plod.

'I'm coming Ping!' screamed Tam, distraught at seeing what had just happened to his old friend.

In one expert, well-practiced motion, Plod drew his sword cane and tossed the sheath to the side. He suddenly came to a stop, swooshed the cane from side to side and stood, planted on his hind legs. He composed himself, adrenaline levels high but without a hint of fear, he narrowed his eyes at the big horn and held the sword, angled to the side with both paws and waited. The big horn charged the brave weasel, towering over him. Within millimetres of contact, Plod was a blur of brown and with a glinting flash from the blade of his sword cane, he sliced a deep wound into one of the big horn's hind legs, spinning skilfully out of the way, ensuring he didn't get trampled in the process. The big horn came crashing to the ground creating vibrations, which made the comrades shake. Plod didn't turn back; he slid the cane back into his belt, minus the sheath and ran over to his friends to check on Ping.

The big horn enraged with pain and anger, wildly shook her head and let out an almighty roar. She started to get up and turned, limping on the deep wound, she once again charged, almost tripping with every step from the gash in her leg. Plod was distracted as he knelt down next to Tam as they tended to Ping. Fortunately, Ping was just bruised and in shock from the sudden attack as they helped her up.

'Ahhhhh!' screamed the small horn in anger. Tam and Plod fell back, surprised as Ping suddenly lurched forward, their eyes widened as they could see the big horn was nearly upon them once again. The big horn went to toss her into the air again, but this time Ping was ready, she easily dodged the attack and ran up her top horn onto her back, sinking her teeth deep into the big horn's neck and using all of her weight as she twisted around, swung herself free from the big horn, landing confidently on all fours. Eyes glazed, the big horn wobbled from side to side and limped straight past Tam and Plod, staggering back to where she came from, deep into Cresswood.

Plod and Tam looked at each other and then to their new recruit open mouthed as she approached them, they all started to laugh, partly from the shock of what had just happened but also out of relief. 'Wow, Ping,' said Plod with a smile, impressed with his new friend's skill in battle. 'Looks like we chose the right small horn for the job.'

'You're not too shabby with that sword cane of yours

either,' replied Ping with a grin as she winced from the painful looking bruises on her side.

'Looks painful, Ping,' remarked Tam as he flew over to his friend to inspect her wounds. 'Lay down, Ping, I'll see to those bruises. I think you may have a few cracked ribs as well.' Tam used his healing magic, closing his eyes he gently laid his hands on to the bruised area, which caused Ping to grimace, passing his energy into the affected area for a couple of minutes. Shortly afterwards, Ping no longer had a look of pain on her face.

'Wow, Tam, thank you,' said Ping with a happy grin on her face. 'I can still see the colouring from the bruises but there is no pain, incredible.'

'No problem, the colouring from the bruising should be gone by morning,' replied Tam, smiling.

'Yep, he has his uses,' chuckled Plod. He patted Tam on the back and winked at Ping as he gathered Pings provisions together, that had scattered about the place, along with his sword cane sheath. Pings provisions were secured back into her wicker pack and Plod slid the sheath over his sword blade. 'Ok guys are we ready to continue?' asked Plod. Tam and Ping agreed, eager to get out of Cresswood and make it to Clamshell Nook before sun went down. Plod slid his sword cane over his back, and they followed Ping once again, heading for the willows and the River Olden.

Chapter 5

They reached the willows by late afternoon and the sun was still beating down. They were grateful to be out of the gloom and danger of Cresswood and amongst the large willows, which were not as densely packed together as the giant cress. Nor did they create a near impenetrable blanket of leaves, reducing the light to create a dim, eerie landscape.

'Ok guys!' shouted Ping from up ahead as she slowed down. 'The river is just up ahead through the willows, we'll come to an old rope bridge and once we cross it, we'll head west for a couple of hours along the river bank until we reach Clamshell Nook.'

'Great, lead on, Ping,' said Plod. They all had a drink from their flasks as they made their way through the beautiful willows, the leaves cascading down to the ground and swaying gently in the breeze. Many of the old willows grew at peculiar angles, creating natural arches for the three comrades to walk under and tiny birds of every colour with long, pointy beaks zipped from tree to tree. They walked at a slower pace now and enjoyed the sight of the little birds and the enchanting willows.

Once they crossed the old rope bridge to the other side of the River Olden, they followed the river along the overgrown path, which was thick with tall grass and wildflowers. After a couple of hours, the sun had started to set, and the fishing village of Clamshell Nook came into view.

'Here we are, Clamshell Nook,' stated Ping. 'Let's see if we can find an inn to start with and get something to eat and secure a room for the night.

'Good idea,' replied Plod. 'I could do with a good meal and maybe we could sound out another member for our party, or at least get an idea of where we should be headed next.' Tam agreed with this plan as they entered Clamshell Nook through a wooden gate on the river bank.

It was a simple fishing village, comprised of sturdy-looking wooden huts with long, sloping roofs, which jutted out a couple of feet from the walls. Many of the chimneys were now sending out faint plumes of smoke as folk began to light their fires. It would get cold once the sun had set and being next to water meant an extra chill came off the river. A long jetty went the length of the village along the river bank and small fishing boats were moored up against the simple wooden dock. There were only a few folk still outside, most had either headed home or gone to get a tankard of beer. The sound of laughter could be heard from a large wooden inn called "Olden's Nook", which was not far from the jetty. A young boy who appeared to be on his own, was tying a boat to a mooring with a frayed old rope. He looked as though he had done it many times before and quickly tied a strong and complex looking knot in a few seconds, securing the small vessel.

'Let's head over to that young lad,' suggested Tam. 'Perhaps he can point us in the direction of a good meal and bed for the night, or maybe his dad can help us.' Plod and Ping nodded, and they headed over to the young boy.

'Hello friend,' said Tam. 'Can we trouble you for a moment?' The boy looked up and eyed the unusual group with curiosity. He seemed especially wary of Tam.

'I didn't think small horns ventured far from their wood?' replied the boy whilst making sure his boat was tight to the mooring. 'And are you ... a scritch of some description? Only ever seen one of your kind before when out fishing the backwaters with my father a few years ago.' The boy sighed and suddenly took on a sad expression, as he looked to the floor for a moment.

'Yes, I am,' replied Tam with a warm, friendly smile. 'A two-footed scritch, unfortunately the three-footed are thought to be extinct many years ago.'

'Do you think we could speak to your father, young man?' added Plod. 'We've had an ... eventful day to say the least and was hoping for bed and board for the night.'

The boy looked to the floor again for a few moments with a sombre look on his face, considering his response, 'I'm afraid ... my father is not around anymore.'

'Oh, will he be back soon?' queried Plod.

'He ... passed away recently,' replied the boy, tears forming in his eyes. 'He became sick and no one in the village was able to help him, he passed away in his sleep.'

Tam and Ping looked to one another, heartbroken by this sad news. 'I ... don't know what to say, young man,' replied Plod, gulping hard, feeling sad for the young boy. 'I'm very sorry for your loss.' Tam flew over to the boy and rested a hand on his shoulder, the powerful energy from Tam's touch helped to put the boy at ease and he gave the group a slight smile.

'Come with me, you can get bed and board at Olden's

Nook Inn. I'll introduce you to the owner, old man Wilbur.' The companions followed the young man over to the warm-looking inn, a roaring fire and lantern light could be seen through the window.

They followed the young boy into the inn, a dozen or so fishermen and residents of Clamshell Nook were sat around tables or at the bar, drinking, eating or playing cards. They didn't seem too concerned by the unusual group that had just entered the bar. Some folk looked up from their beers and then carried on laughing and being merry with their friends. Mr Wilbur was cleaning a tankard and eyed the group, he beckoned the young boy over with a friendly but inquiring smile, wondering who the boy's new friends were.

They followed the boy up to the bar. 'Made some new friends, Brillo?' asked Wilbur in a deep but friendly voice, nodding to the group. He was a man of later years, tall and stocky with a thick white beard and not a single hair on his head. Deep lines in his face created shadows, which gave him quite a menacing appearance, although he had a welcoming and friendly way about him.

'They approached me out by my mooring, they've had a hard day's travel and need bed and board for the night. Wilbur, can you accommodate them?' inquired the boy, on the party's behalf.

'Aye, I'm sure I can sort something out, lad,' replied Wilbur, he turned to the group. 'We only have a few rooms but the largest is unoccupied, it also has three beds, if you're happy sharing it's yours for the night. It will be two coins for bed and board, it would usually be one a piece, but as you've come in with Brillo here, I'm happy to do it for two. If you take your things up to the room, I'll have cook rustle you up something to eat and you can all have a tankard of strome mead on the house.' Strome mead was a popular beer, drunk all over Wilstrome and was made from the native strome berry, which gave the beer a deep, dark red colour once brewed.

The friends all looked to each other and grinned. 'Thank you, Wilbur,' replied Plod. 'That would be most kind, we'll take our packs up to the room now, if that's OK?' The currency across Wilstrome consisted of small, unmarked gold coins. Plod took two gold coins from his pack and paid for the room. Wilbur thanked him and asked the young boy if he could show the travellers to their lodgings.

Once the boy had shown them to their room for the night, they threw their packs on the beds and headed back downstairs, eager for a meal and a tankard of cold strome mead. 'Would you eat with us ... Brillo, is it?' asked Tam.

'Yes, my name is actually, Benjamin Brillo, but everyone around here just calls me, Brillo. I usually eat on alone in my hut which is opposite the inn. Wilbur always says I'm welcome to a free hot meal, he has sort of looked out for me ... ever since dad ... he was good friends with my father.' Brillo trailed off as he spoke, his thoughts going elsewhere.

'Great!' replied Ping, before Brillo had time to give a proper answer. 'That's settled then, you can show us the best seats in the inn.' Brillo grinned as Plod gave him a friendly tap on the arm with his paw. He was not really sure what to make of this interesting band of travellers, but he couldn't help but like them, they seemed like genuine, good folk.

Brillo was a tall for his age, lean and healthy 12-year-old boy, with short, scruffy black hair and pale blue eyes. He wore his late father's tatty, old, light brown round-brimmed fishing hat that had picked up a few tears over the years. His brown knee length shorts and white short sleeved shirt were equally as tatty and well-worn and his leather sandals had faded to a washed-out light brown colour, from the constant exposure to sun and river water. He took the companions over to the fire place in the corner of the inn. 'This is my favourite spot,' stated Brillo. 'It's usually quiet and I like to just come and sit and watch the fire from time to time.' A sturdy oak table and four chairs were set a few feet away from the crackling fire.

The companions smiled at each other, pleased with young Brillo's choice. 'Perfect,' said Plod. 'I'll go and tell Wilbur we're ready for our meals.' As Plod went to get up, the cook appeared from a door to the side of the bar and brought out their food and tankards of beer, including a plate for Brillo and small glass of strome mead. Wilbur looked over to them and raised his hand. They all raised their glasses to him and smiled as they thanked him for his hospitality, he grinned and winked at Brillo, then went back to cleaning his tankards and serving at the bar.

They all got stuck into their meals of roast potatoes, vegetables and thick steaks of some sort, possibly rift elk. A species of large, powerful deer that are native to the Riftbrook area of Wilstrome. 'So, Brillo,' started Plod as he chewed on steak and took a hearty swig of his cold strome mead. 'You looked like you knew what you were doing, tying that mooring knot earlier? You're a fisherman then?'

'Yes,' replied Brillo, sipping at his small glass of beer. 'When dad passed, I took over the business. Fortunately, he had started teaching me how to fish and handle the boat as soon as I could walk, so I know what I'm doing on the water. My father's father was a fisherman and his father and so on, we have always fished.'

The friends nodded as they enjoyed their food, interested in the young boy's story and impressed with his mature attitude. 'Do you have any help with the boat, Brillo?' asked Tam.

'No, unfortunately I'm on my own now, as mum passed away when I was born, leaving just me and my dad. Wilbur is like family though; I suppose he is like an uncle to me. He was always very good friends with dad. I like to keep busy and although hard, I prefer to work the boat alone.'

'Very impressive, Brillo,' said Ping. 'You sound as though you work extremely hard, I'm sure your mother and father would be incredibly proud of you.' Plod and Tam nodded in agreement.

'Thank you, Ping,' replied Brillo with a half-smile, blushing slightly at Ping's comments. 'What brings you three out to the little fishing village of Clamshell Nook?' inquired Brillo.

'We're actually looking for someone,' replied Plod. 'Anyone in fact, who would be suitable to join our party. We have an extremely important quest to undertake for the good of Wilstrome and need to recruit members to our band. I won't trouble you with all the details, but do you happen to know of any brave souls with previous experience of undertaking dangerous quests by any chance?'

'Wow, sounds mysterious,' replied Brillo, raising his eyebrows, intrigued. 'Unfortunately, I don't think you will find anyone around here, it's just a simple fishing village. The inhabitants are quiet folk who have lived here all their lives, they're not really interested in adventure.' 'Oh, really?' replied Plod, looking to his two friends, somewhat disheartened by these words.

'Although, I may know somewhere not too far from here,' replied Brillo. The three friends all quickly looked up from their food, the young boy now piquing their interest. 'A large aqua town called Oden's Moat can be found about half a day's boat trip, down the River Olden. Aqua towns are entirely on the river, all the houses are built on large stilts in the water or on floating pontoons. It's the largest aqua town I have ever visited and probably the biggest in all of Wilstrome. Many rivers and streams flow into Olden's Moat and its only accessible by boat, but fortunately, we are on the banks of the River Olden, which is one of the largest main rivers in Wilstrome. So, we are well placed to visit the town.'

The three friends looked intrigued by Brillo's suggestion of Olden's Moat. 'Brillo, would you be interested in providing us with transport to Oldens Moat? Obviously, we would pay you well for your time and expertise,' inquired Plod.

'Hmm,' Brillo considered Plod's request, tapping a finger on his top lip as though he was thinking about it. Plod gave an unsure look to his friends, thinking that Brillo was about to turn down his request. 'Yes, I would love to, Plod, it would be my pleasure. Anything that gets me out of the village for a bit - even if it isn't a proper adventure – sounds good to me. When do we leave, first light sound good for you guys?'

'Ha!' screeched Tam in excitement. 'Fantastic news, Brillo, thank you,' Tam was instinctively about to perform his victory lap without thinking, but Plod and Ping grabbed on to him, chuckling, and stopped him. Brillo burst into laughter with his new friends - they were pleased to see him happy.

'Yes, first light sounds great Brillo,' agreed Plod. 'We'll meet you at your mooring first thing.' The four companions finished their meals in front of the crackling fire and Brillo sipped on his beer. The others ordered another round of beer. Once finished, they thanked Brillo for his help and made their way up to their room to get a good night's sleep, whilst Brillo returned to his hut, opposite the Olden's Nook Inn.

The three companions awoke before first light, excited for the trip via boat to the large aqua town, Oldens Moat. Once Plod had strapped on his sword cane, they gathered their packs together and went downstairs. They placed the packs beside the fire, and they sat in the same spot as the night before. It was chilly morning, but Wilbur had been up early to light the fire. He brought over some tankards of water and two plates of food, one piled high with thick, crusty buttered bread and the other with fresh fruit.

'Morning travellers,' said Wilbur in his deep, warm voice. 'I don't usually get up this early, Brillo came over earlier and woke me, he said he was providing you with transport to Olden's Moat. Brillo doesn't usually travel far from his mooring, he's quite excited.' Wilbur threw another log on the fire; it was giving off a fair amount of heat now. 'I thought I would get the fire going and make sure you're well fed before the journey.

'Thank you,' said Tam, happily. 'You've both been very kind.'

'It's no bother,' replied Wilbur. 'We don't get many travellers passing through here. I think it will be good for Brillo to do something a bit different for a day or so. He's like a son to me really, I don't have any of my own but that's how I see him ... especially since his father passed away. He seemed to enjoy spending time with you all here last night though, so I thank you for that.'

The friends listened intently to his words. 'He did seem very excited about the trip last night, Wilbur, I'm sure he will enjoy himself,' replied Plod as he took a large piece of crusty bread from the plate.

They all ate a good breakfast and gathered their packs. Before leaving, they thanked Wilbur for his hospitality and said they hoped they would be able to visit again soon.

They left the Olden's Nook Inn and walked over to Brillo's mooring, he was already checking over the boat and packing some water and provisions for the trip. 'Hello fellow sailors!' shouted Brillo, smiling and waving to them as they walked over.

'I'm impressed, Brillo,' said Ping. 'It looks like you're ready to leave. Is there anything we can help you with?'

'Nope, we're all set, Ping,' replied Brillo. 'Throw your packs up and jump aboard.' They threw their packs up to Brillo and he stacked them in a wooden trunk located along the length of the deck at the stern, which also acted as a seat. A winch was also fitted to the stern of the boat, a thick rope was wound around the winch and attached to an anchor. It was a small 20ft wooden fishing boat with a mainsail and small front jib sail. The front of the boat had a little cabin with windows to the front and side and a large wooden wheel in the centre. A couple of cupboards stood on either side of the cabin, topped with bedrolls to act as simple beds and a candle lantern swung from the cabin roof.

Plod and Ping jumped onto the deck, Tam jumped and gave a single flap of his wings, gliding onto the deck. 'We're all aboard and ready to leave, Brillo,' said Plod. Brillo nodded to his new shipmates and jumped off the boat onto the jetty. He untied his mooring rope and threw it onto the deck. He gave one big push of the boat and then leaped on before it was too far to make the jump. The boat slowly drifted out into the centre of the large river and Brillo raised his sails, he set the wheel in the cabin, so the boat was steadily headed down the river, in the direction of Olden's Moat. They all waved goodbye to Wilbur who was standing outside the Olden's Nook.

After a couple of hours of making good progress in the little sailing boat, Brillo noticed something in the distance, 'We have a problem, guys,' said Brillo whilst staring out the front cabin window. The others walked into the cabin and jumped up onto the cabinets and looked out the window. 'A massive tree has blown down, blocking the river. We've had some pretty bad storms in the last couple of weeks, it must have happened pretty recently as no one has mentioned anything about a fallen tree.'

'Oh, does that mean it's not possible to make it into Olden's Moat, Brillo?' asked Ping.

'Well … we could always take a backwater stream, I suppose,' replied Brillo, cautiously. 'One is just coming up on the left, it's just about big enough to take the boat. It's the only one before we reach the fallen tree, otherwise it's a long way back down the river to the next one.'

'You don't sound too sure about the stream,' queried Plod. 'Is there something troubling you about this alternate route?'

'It's wise to always avoid all backwater streams, if possible, guys,' replied Brillo. 'They are home to outlaws and thieves, primarily the thief-kind, a dangerous species. My father always taught me to avoid the streams unless absolutely necessary. This may be one of those times though, backtracking would add a massive amount of time onto our journey, and I get the impression, time isn't on your side with this quest.'

'Unfortunately, you are correct, young Brillo,' said Plod. 'I don't want to put you in any unnecessary danger. If you wish to head back then that's what we'll do and there will be no hard feelings with your decision.'

'Thief-kind or no thief-kind, I'm taking you guys to Olden's Moat,' stated Brillo. 'We take the backwaters.' With the decision made, the brave young fisherman from Clamshell Nook slowed his boat and started to angle it so he could enter the mouth of a small stream up ahead. Once he entered the stream, he had to be careful as jagged looking rocks poked out of the water and branches from trees and bushes overhung the banks of the stream and brushed against the boat. They slowly made their way down the stream, Brillo was deep in concentration as he expertly threaded his vessel past any obstructions.

They weren't alone, shortly after entering the stream they had been followed, stealthily along the bank through the thick tangle of trees and undergrowth. 'Plod!' hissed Brillo, Plod quickly entered the cabin, followed by Tam and Ping. 'We're not alone!' He kept his voice low.

Plod peered out the window, he could just about make out movement through the undergrowth, whoever they were, they were dressed in dark clothing and slipped effortlessly and silently through the trees. 'Thief-kind?' asked Plod in a whisper. Tam and Ping glanced cautiously out the window, feeling their hearts start to race.

'Most likely,' replied Brillo. 'I'm going to speed up, we need to make it to Olden's Moat, fast.' Brillo quickly ran out of the cabin and raised his mainsail. Up to this point, he had just been using the boat's small jib sail to slowly sail down the narrow stream. The wind was behind them and the boat quickly started to pick up alarming speed on the small backwater. It seemed the groups stalkers had already allowed for this scenario and they no longer worried about being seen, realising they had been spotted. A shout of "Set the rope!" could be heard from the bank next to them. Up ahead, a couple of darkly dressed individuals could be seen pulling hard on an extremely thick rope and securing it in place around a large rock. 'That rope will destroy the hull!' shouted Brillo. 'I'm going to have to lower the sails and bring the boat to a stop, sorry, we'll have to see what they want.'

'OK, Brillo, we don't want to destroy the boat, try and stay calm,' reassured Plod as he instinctively touched the hilt of his sword cane.

Brillo dropped his anchor and came to a halt a few yards from the rope blocking their path. 'Are you lost out here in the backwaters, Boy!' shouted one of the thief-kind from the bank, his voice an unpleasant cackle. The thief-kind could very nearly be mistaken for humans although you can usually spot them due to a few small details. They are very lean and slender folk, rarely exceeding 4.5ft in height and creep with a slightly hunched-over gait. They tend to have odd numbers of long, bony fingers and toes on their hands and feet and a natural disposition towards crime and the underworld. They always dressed in rugged, well-worn black and brown clothing with a hood, keeping their thin, angular faces shadowy and dark.

'We're headed to Olden's Moat!' shouted Brillo confidently, the others were at his side and Plod was ready to draw his cane if necessary.

'How strange, you won't be able to make it to Olden's Moat without a boat!' replied the outlaw. Three thief-kind were standing on the bank, the one doing the talking was standing in the middle of them, standing slightly forward. Two more thief-kind prowled out of the undergrowth and stood next to them, they all had crooked grins on their faces.

'OK ... there's five of them now guys,' whispered Plod. 'I was comfortable with three ... what shall we do? They're all armed and the two at the back have loaded crossbows.' The three at the front of the group had sabres hanging from sword belts at their sides and the two at the rear were ready with their crossbows.

'OK, you can board we don't want any trouble!' shouted Brillo.

'Good lad, you and your friends get to live another

day, now leave all your things, that includes the cane on your back, weasel!' shouted the outlaw. The outlaws dropped a plank onto the deck, which acted as a gangway onto the bank.

'You guys leave first, very slowly,' whispered Brillo to the group as he knelt down.

His companions looked at him with confusion. 'What's the plan?' whispered Plod as he removed his belt and sword cane, placing it on the wooden trunk seat at the rear of the boat.

'I don't have time to explain, just take your time, try and distract them,' replied Brillo. As the others slowly made their way over to the plank, Brillo spread out a large, strong looking fishing net on the deck of the boat. He glanced over to his new friends and the thief-kind. Plod and Ping were making a meal out of walking the gangway, pretending to wobble all over the place which made the outlaws laugh. Tam flew about spiralling through the air behind them, which distracted the thief-kind as they had to keep an eye on the unusual creature. Brillo quickly weaved strong, clear fishing line through the top of the net. As soon as the thief-kind where all distracted, he stood up and threw the spool of line accurately over a small wooden beam which jutted out at the top of the mast. He skilfully flung the spool hard over the heads of the thief-kind and it landed in some long grass a few yards behind them. They didn't notice, but Plod and ping saw the spool quietly drop onto the grass behind the outlaws, they were still confused at what their new friend had up his sleeve.

Plod and Ping reached the bank. 'Come on boy, what's taking so long? We want to use our new boat!' cackled the outlaw.

Brillo swiftly made his way over to the makeshift gangway, 'Sorry, I just wanted to say one last goodbye to my boat,' replied Brillo, putting on his saddest face.

'Ahhhh, how sad, did you here that lads - better get your handkerchiefs at the ready - the boy was saying "goodbye" to his boat!' The outlaws fell about laughing, pretending to cry and dry their eyes. Brillo walked onto the bank and stood next to his friends as the outlaws gave a bow and waved their hands, mocking them as they boarded the small vessel. They all stood on the middle of the deck, the two with the crossbows placed them on the trunk at the stern and they didn't think anything of the net, it was a fishing boat after all. They continued to mock the companions, gesturing sad faces. As they did this, Brillo darted over to the spool of line, which was lying on the long grass behind them. 'Hey! What do you think you're doing lad?' queried one of the thief-kind, his laughter slipping to an unsure smirk, the other outlaws stopped their ridicule as well and stared at the boy.

Brillo's new comrades watched him with interest, they were as confused as the thief-kind. He grabbed the spool and held it triumphantly above his head. 'Well, well, well, lads,' Brillo began, 'Thank you for kindly laying your loaded crossbows on my trunk, this is genuinely, much appreciated.' The thief-kind looked to each other, confused, a look of concern spreading across their faces. Brillo yanked hard on the spool, whilst running backwards down the bank of the stream and the net shot up around all five of the thief-kind.

'Arrghh!' The outlaws shrieked and cried out as they fell over one another in a tangle, trapped in the fishing net.

Brillo's comrades had satisfied grins as they watched

the scene unfold and they punched the air. 'Haha! That'll show em, Brillo!' shouted Plod.

'Take this for me and keep it tight,' Brillo handed the spool to plod and with the help of Tam and Ping they kept the line tight. Brillo sprinted up the gangway and climbed halfway up the small mainsail mast so he was above the net, he took a penknife from his pocket and seemingly, in one expert motion, cut the line and tied a secure knot.

The outlaws were in an uncomfortable looking tangle of arms and legs. 'What do you think you're doing, boy!' shrieked one of the outlaws in pain as a knee pressed hard into his face. 'let us go now and we won't kill you! Let us go! Now!'

At that moment, Plod somersaulted onto the deck and drew his sword cane from its sheath, he thrust it with lightning speed, stopping a millimetre from the outlaw's eye. Ping and Tam picked up the loaded crossbows and aimed them at the outlaws. 'What did you have to say to my friend here?' demanded Plod with anger in his voice, narrowing his eyes at the outlaw. 'I didn't quite catch that, please repeat your words.' The outlaw could see that the weasel meant business and calling his bluff wouldn't end well.

The writhing around in the net stopped, knowing that they were in a helpless situation. 'OK, weasel, calm down, let's talk about this in a civilised manner,' said the outlaw, his voice breaking with fear.

'I think we're beyond "civilised", don't you?' added Ping. Tam couldn't help but grin at the sudden change of fortune and let out a chuckle before composing himself.

Brillo took a rope from the wooden trunk at the rear of the boat and looped it through the net, making a strong knot. 'OK guys, help me remove these unwelcome idiots from my boat please!' yelled Brillo. All four of them pulled on the rope and dragged the entangled thief-kind down the gangway and onto the bank.

'Please!' pleaded one of the desperate outlaws. 'You can't just leave us here, what if no one comes past! It's a remote area!'

The four friends walked back up the gangway onto the deck. 'I'll be taking your gangway, oh and your cross-bows, I do hope that's OK? A fair trade for one of my fishing nets, wouldn't you say?' said Brillo with a wicked grin. The others all smirked as they stood on the deck, impressed with the young fisherman's handling of the outlaws.

'Noooo! We'll kill you! You won't get away with this!' cried the outlaws, writhing around in the net.

'Yeah, we will,' replied Plod, flatly, completely un-fazed by their threats as he slid his sword back into its sheath. 'OK guys, onwards to Olden's Moat then?' Brillo smiled and raised the jib sail, they gently set off back down the stream and continued on to their destination.

The angry shouts and threats from the thief-kind quickly faded out of earshot. Brillo skilfully sailed the boat down the stream, avoiding anything that could damage the hull. The aqua town of Olden's Moat came into view a couple of hours after leaving the defeated outlaws on the bank of the stream.

Chapter 6

T hey left the backwater stream, having completed their perilous trip through the dense, knotted woods that flowed into the town. Brillo gently eased the boat over to the dock. A series of long, floating, wooden jetties, all in organised lines in the middle of the town and many boats of various types, shapes and sizes were moored up there. Fishing vessels many times larger than Brillo's small craft were moored beside paddle steamers and rowing boats next to grand looking sail boats. The group were so captivated by all the assorted craft, they nearly didn't spot the unusual looking fellow waving them over to a free mooring spot.

'That's us,' said Brillo, taking the boat as near to the mooring as he could. He lowered the jib sail and ran over to his mooring rope; he threw it over to the fellow on the jetty and he pulled them in tight, tying the rope to the mooring post. Plod, Tam and Ping stood on the boats deck and stared at the interesting town, it was the first time they had visited Olden's Moat and they seemed lost in their thoughts. Brillo chuckled at his friends, he had already made use of his newly acquired gangway plank and was waiting on the jetty for them. 'Hey, shipmates, over here!' Brillo waved to them and laughed.

'Oh, sorry, Brillo, come on guys,' replied Tam. They took their packs and Plod strapped on his belt and sword cane. He placed Brillo's newly acquired crossbows in the boat's wooden trunk and tapped the top with his paw, hoping that Brillo wouldn't ever need to use them.

Plod was the final member of the team to make it across the plank and Brillo pushed it back onto the deck when they were all safely across. They all glanced around for a moment, taking in the sights and smells of the large town. It had been a couple of years since Brillo was last there, with his late father. As well as boats constantly mooring, they were also setting off, leaving the town and heading down one of the streams or rivers that flowed into Olden's Moat. Many of the buildings sat on tall stilts that towered above them; they stood and stared from the floating jetty at water level. Others were perched on floating pontoons, dotted around the town. You could taste, as well as smell the wood smoke hanging in the air. Plumes of smoke pumped out of the numerous houses, inns, and workshops. The sound of metal hitting metal and wood being sawn, created a constant background noise, which mixed with folk shouting and laughing and the commotion of boats arriving and leaving. The jetty they had moored at, led straight down to a large pontoon, housing a floating boatyard and steep wooden staircases on either side led up to the stilt buildings above. The whole town was connected by wooden walkways with handrails on either side, which bridged one stilted section to the other. Staircases would lead down to the lower water level areas and stop a foot or so above the many floating jetties, which led down the pontoon buildings, as well as the boat moorings.

'Right then, Brillo,' said Ping. 'Lead on, let's see if we

can find somewhere to have a good meal and a comfy bed for the night.' They all agreed and followed Brillo down the jetty to the boatyard, taking the stairs up to the stilt level buildings. The sun had begun to set, and a chill was in the air. If it weren't for the unforeseen setback with the thief-kind, Brillo would have made the round trip in one day, but it would be getting dark soon.

'Don't mind me sharing a room for the night, do you?' asked Brillo as he led them over a wooden bridge past some timber houses and a little hut selling freshly caught fish.

'Of course not,' assured Plod. 'I wouldn't have you go back in this light and there's still the issue of that fallen tree on the main river. We need to work out how you can return safely to Clamshell Nook. For the meantime, though, let's get sat in front of a fire with a tankard of strome mead and a tasty meal'

'I'm going to take us to the Flying Pike Inn,' said Brillo. 'I used to go there with my father on the odd occasion we ventured this far, and they also provide bed and board.' As they moved deeper into the maze of stilt buildings, walkways and narrow bridges, they could hear some sort of commotion up ahead.

'Ahhhrg! Please! This is my home! I have nowhere else to go!' The unusual fellow - who looked similar to the helpful dock worker that helped moor their boat earlier – had just been thrown out of a house. He skidded along the wooden walkway and narrowly avoided falling over the side.

'Oh! let's see what trouble this gillsprog has gotten into,' stated Brillo. Plod looked blankly to Ping and Tam and mouthed, "gillsprog?", they shrugged at each other and followed close behind Brillo as they approached the creature. 'What seems to be the matter? Are you OK?' asked Brillo as he held out a hand to the gillsprog.

'No ... not really,' replied the distressed gillsprog in a squeaky, high-pitched voice. He took Brillo's hand. 'Thank you, young man, that's very good of you.' The creature looked quite dishevelled. He wore tattered, beige three quarter length trousers and a wrinkled, white short sleeved shirt.

As Brillo helped the gillsprog to his feet, a couple of shady looking characters who appeared to be thief-kind came to the front door, 'You lost fair and square, Tog! Barked the cackling outlaw. 'Now don't let me find you around here again, it would probably be best if you left Olden's Moat, for good!'

'My home!' cried Tog as he put his head in his webbed hands.

Tam was concerned for the gillsprog and flew over to him resting a hand on his shoulder, 'It's Tog, isn't it?' asked Tam, calming him slightly. Tog nodded. 'What's happened here?'

'I've been a fool! It's all my own fault, so stupid, I've been ... reckless,' whimpered Tog as he began to explain the situation. 'I've lost everything I own, including my home and all my coin due to my ... gambling. I lost a high stakes game – and when I say, "high stakes", I mean every-thing – of 52 card switch. There were eight of us in the game and I imagine everyone other than me were work-ing together on the same side.' Tog once again buried his head in his hands. 'Why would I bet everything against scoundrels and thieves,' he mumbled. The incredibly complex game of 52 card switch is favoured by rogues and outlaws the realm over for its suitability in trick-ing and swindling unsuspected newcomers to the game.

Even veteran players have been caught out by groups of scoundrels working as one to fleece their marks.

'Why don't you join us at the Flying Pike?' asked Brillo. 'Were headed there now to seek bed and board.'

'I really wouldn't want to burden you,' mumbled Tog.

'Come on now,' said Plod, assertively. 'You're coming with us; we're not leaving you on the floor here to wallow. I'll get you a tankard of strome mead and a warm meal.'

'You're more than welcome to join us, Tog,' added Ping, giving the gillsprog a friendly smile.

'Really?' replied Tog. 'I don't know what to say, thank you, weasel, you're all very kind.'

Brillo led the way as his new companions, including the down-on-his-luck gillsprog, Tog, followed him over to the large inn, called the Flying Pike, which was five minutes' walk from Tog's commandeered house.

The inn was busy, and many different species were enjoying drinking and eating together and being merry. Dwarves, humans, gillsprogs, even the odd weasel and to Ping's surprise, a small horn cress mite could be seen in the hustle and bustle of the inn, laughing and discussing their day. They definitely wouldn't be out of place in this town.

'Follow me,' said Tog. 'There is a table in a secluded corner that has its own wood burner, it's usually free as it's always a bit dark and dingy. I eh … have played one or two games of cards in this spot,'

They followed Tog over to his favourite table, it was empty, just like he suggested it would be. He took a pack of matches from behind the burner and got it going, the dark corner was now lit with warm, shadowy light. He pulled up the required number of chairs around the small table and they all sat down, stacking their packs, along with Plod's sword cane, neatly in the corner opposite the wood burner.

'Hmm, cosy, I like it, Tog,' observed Tam.

Just as they were getting comfortable a young gill-sprog made her way over to take their order. Gillsprogs are a local water dwelling species, which usually live their entire lives on the water. They can be found in all aqua towns and they very rarely head onto land unless they absolutely have to. Adults reach a height of no more than 4ft and they are similar to frogs in appearance, except they walk upright on their hind legs and they have large, webbed feet and hands and are extremely proficient swimmers. Their glistening skin has light shades of green and blue and they have wide, over-sized heads with external gills and large black eyes. 'Hey Tog, not playing cards today?' inquired the cheerful gillsprog.

'I eh … not today, Pip' replied Tog. 'Just showing these weary travellers here the best inn in town, they require bed and board for the night if you have any room?'

'Hello travellers, why, hello there scritch, it's been a long time since I have seen your kind around here, it's a pleasure to meet you,' said Pip in a cheery, welcoming demeanour. Tam chuckled and gave his little bow. 'Yes, we do have a few large rooms available, how many beds do you require?'

'I think … five would be sufficient,' replied Tam, quickly, before anyone else could answer. He looked at Plod and glanced quickly in Tog's direction. Plod narrowed his eyebrows at his friend, unsure whether he really wanted someone who appeared so reckless and untrustworthy staying in a room with them.

'No problem,' replied Pip. 'Are you still waiting on

someone then?' she queried, wondering why they needed five beds when they had a party of four.

'No, we're not waiting on anyone … we usually prefer a room with the extra space to store our equipment,' answered Ping.

'Ahh, OK, that makes sense,' replied Pip with a smile. 'If you just pay for the room to secure it, you can settle up your food and drinks bill in the morning before you leave. It would usually be five coins, one each, but as it's actually just four of you and Tog here has recommended the Pike, you can have the room for four coins'

'Thank you, that's very kind,' replied Plod as he found his coin pouch in his pack. When his back was turned to Pip, he shot Tam a glance, raising an eyebrow, Tam returned a slightly nervous looking smile. 'Here you are, four coins,' stated Plod as he dropped the coins one-by-one into the Pip's webbed hand.

'Great, thank you, weasel,' replied Pip. 'I imagine you could all do with a nice cold tankard of strome mead - can I also recommend the rift elk pie with vegetables?' They all looked to one another, grinned and nodded enthusiastically in Pip's direction.

After a few minutes, four tankards of strome mead and a smaller half-sized tankard came out for the travellers, including Tog. Ten minutes after the drinks were served, five large plates were brought out, each with a mountain of roasted, mixed vegetables and a huge, thick, crusty rift elk pie. Brillo took a hearty sip on his small tankard of strome mead and held the drink up to toast the group. 'Thanks, Plod, I feel like I could eat an entire rift elk.' They all agreed and held their tankards up, chuckling at Brillo's comment.

'Thank you so much for this, guys,' said Tog, looking genuinely pleased to be shown such generosity. 'You must have a lot of equipment to take up to your room, I'm happy to help, it's the least I can do,' offered Tog, not realising the extra bed was for him.

'The extra bed isn't due to our equipment, Tog,' Replied Tam with a warm smile. 'It's for you, so you have somewhere to stay for the night.'

A tear rolled down Tog's cheek, he was overcome with emotion. He had not been shown much kindness in his life and didn't expect any from complete strangers. 'I ... I don't know what to say ... thank you so much for this,' said the emotional gillsprog.

Plod's general uneasiness towards the idea of Tog staying in their room started to slip when he could see his genuine appreciation for their help. 'No, that's quite alright, Tog,' said Plod, giving a Tam a quick half-smile.

'What will you do, Tog?' asked Ping with a look of concern on her face for the homeless gillsprog. 'Do you have friends you will be able to stay with after tonight?'

Tog put his head in his hands again, clearly very distressed by this thought, 'No, not really. Pip would probably allow me to stay at the Pike for a few days if I had to, her parents own this inn. I wouldn't want to burden them though and I'm not welcome in Olden's Moat anymore, not now the thief-kind want me to leave ... I haven't got a clue what I'll do.' He started to trail off into a mumble as he began to sob. The group looked to one another, concerned for Tog, Tam put a hand on his shoulder and tried to calm him.

'Why, eh ... doesn't Tog join your band, Plod?' queried Brillo as he chewed though a large mouthful of pie.

Plod was unsure by Brillo's idea, but Ping and Tam looked pleadingly in his direction, he could see how much distress the gillsprog was in and felt some responsibility for him. 'Tog, do you think you could bring anything to our little band here?' asked Plod, hesitantly. 'We are on a perilous quest and success isn't guaranteed.'

Tog's head shot up and he wiped the tears from his large eyes, 'Really, Plod, I could join your party? Yes, Yes I would love too!' replied Tog enthusiastically. 'I would even be happy to travel overland. Us gillsprogs are excellent swimmers. I'm also a good problem solver, I realise taking on, no less than seven obvious crooks single-handedly at 52 card switch was a ... slight misjudgement, but I do believe I could be another valuable member to your current team of four.'

'It's actually just three of us,' replied Plod. 'Young Brillo here kindly gave us safe passage from Clamshell nook.'

'About that, Plod,' said Brillo. 'I don't suppose you have room for the two of us in your party?'

Tam and Ping shot each other excited looks and Tam was dangerously close to performing his victory lap around the inn. 'Well, Brillo, you're an extremely competent, skilled boatman and we were all astonished with how quick-witted you were earlier, taking care of those outlaws ... but you're still young and what about Wilbur?' asked Plod with a serious expression.

'I'm the master of my own destiny now, Plod,' replied Brillo. 'Wilbur will understand, I want to find adventure and see what's beyond the village.'

Plod's serious expression slipped, and he couldn't help but smile, 'Let me at least explain the details of this quest to you both and then you can decide if you really want to join. If your answer is still yes, then we would be happy to have you both,' he said, looking from Brillo to

Tog. Plod looked around and hunched over, taking care that he would not be overheard, shadows flickered over his face from the light of the wood burner as the others leaned in. They listened carefully as he explained to the two potential new recruits the gravity of the quest they would be embarking on.

'Wow, this isn't your average quest, this could change Wilstrome forever,' said Brillo once Plod had explained what they would be getting themselves in to. 'I thought the ... beast was slain when you last fought it, Plod?' continued Brillo in a hushed tone. 'Either that or folk believe it had left the mountains, never to return.

'Well, as I explained,' replied Plod. 'My band fought until I was the only one left. The beast staggered off, deep into the mountains and I only just managed to make my way down, where I blacked out. If it weren't for Tam and his healing magic I would have died.' Tam gave his friend a sombre smile, remembering that fateful day. 'I'm afraid the re-emergence of the beast is confirmed by the town and village leaders who proposed this quest. They have had confirmed sightings, and the strange disappearance of farm animals close to the mountains also provides more evidence.'

'Like I said, I want to find adventure and see what's beyond the village,' stated Brillo. 'No matter how dangerous the quest. Maybe it's fate, or maybe it's just pure coincidence, but you can count on me.'

Plod, Tam and Ping looked at the young boy, impressed. He was brave, intelligent and knew his own mind, clearly, nothing would stop him. They knew they could count on young Brillo.

Tog had a dumbstruck impression and appeared to be lost in his thoughts, staring at the flames licking the glass panel of the wood burner.

'Tog?' said Brillo. 'What do you think? Are you OK? You seem to be deep in thought, are you going to join the party with me?'

'I … eh, the Skinkadink,' said Tog as the others hushed him, not wanting anyone to overhear talk of the foul creature. He suddenly snapped out of his fog, 'Sorry about that, guys. I've never done anything courageous in my life, foolish maybe, but not exactly courageous. As much as the thought of going up against that creature terrifies me, I think I need to do something … good, or at least it will be if we actually succeed. Yes … yes you can count me in, I promise, I will give you my best.'

The group could see that Tog had given this thought and he was sincere, if not a bit apprehensive, but that was to be expected. 'Welcome aboard, looks like we have two new members to our little band of adventurers,' said Plod with a grin, holding out his paw to shake their hands.

'Tam!' chuckled Ping 'not in here!' Plod and Ping lurched over to their friend and grabbed onto his feet to stop his victory lap around the busy inn.

'Oh, I am sorry,' apologised Tam with a cheeky grin. 'I just get overexcited sometimes, welcome to the team!'

They all ordered another tankard of strome mead each to celebrate, and once finished gathered their packs and headed up to the room, eager to get a good night's sleep and continue the quest as a band of five.

∞∞∞

Brillo and Tog were up at first light, excited and anxious to be on a quest to defeat the Skinkadink. They sat in the same spot as the night before and got the wood burner going to take the chill off the early morning air, they were the only folk in the inn. Shortly after, the others came down and spotted them stoking the burner, they all took their seats around the table and waited for someone to serve breakfast.

They didn't have to wait long; Pip came out looking tired but still wore her cheery smile, 'Why hello travellers, I see you've made some new friends, Tog, bit early for you isn't it?'

'I'm actually leaving, Pip,' replied Tog. 'I'm not sure when, if ever, I'll return, I'm ... going to work on their fishing boat and see more of Wilstrome, outside of Olden's Moat.'

'Oh, I'll be sorry to see you leave, Tog,' replied Pip, her smile slipping. 'I think a bit of adventure will be good for you though, Tog, anything to get you away from the cards.' She shot him a knowing but friendly glance and her warm smile spread back across her face.

Tog blushed slightly, 'Thank you, Pip.'

'What can I get you brave adventurers then?' asked Pip.

The five companions grinned at each other; Pip didn't realise how accurate her words were. 'Whatever you think would give five fishermen enough energy for a hard day's work, please.' said Plod, still smiling.

Five minutes later, Pip came out with a mountain of

crusty, fried egg rolls and an equally large plate of mixed fruits. She placed two large jugs of water on the table and laid out five tankards.

'This looks wonderful, Pip,' said Tam. 'Thank you.' The others agreed and they eagerly took a mound of egg rolls and fresh fruit.

'Where are we headed next then, guys?' inquired Ping, before chomping into a well-filled egg roll.

'Good question,' replied Plod. 'We could do with a couple more members to our party. Any more would remove the element of stealth, which we will require when hunting the Skinkadink. It doesn't have the best sense of smell, but it does have excellent vision, it's a sight hunter. Ideally, we could do with a couple of hunters or warriors skilled in the use of blade or bow.'

'Eagles Breath,' replied Tog, quickly, with a full mouth as he enjoyed his breakfast.

'Good idea, Tog,' agreed Plod. 'It's been a long time since I've visited Eagles Breath, but it has a long tradition of supplying adventurers for hire throughout its many inns and adventurer's guilds. How far is it though, in relation to Olden's Moat?'

The others looked blankly at each other, having never heard of the town before. 'The quickest route,' started Tog. 'Would be to take the River Olden, north, it's a large town situated next to the river so we can moor up on the bank. There is a place there called the Guild & Inn, it literally serves as an adventurer's guild and an inn. I know it well as I played a game of cards there once ... that was one of my more successful endeavours.'

'That's sorted then, I'll go and ready the boat,' said Brillo, eager to set off.

'I'll come and help you, Brillo,' added Tog.

'Eagles Breath it is then,' confirmed Plod. 'We'll get our things from the room and I'll settle up our bill and meet you at the boat in twenty minutes.' Brillo and Tog had finished their breakfast, so they made their way over to the mooring spot.

Brillo was carefully checking over his boat, concerned that the hull may have been damaged in yesterday's eventful trip down the backwater stream. Tog had set the gangway plank so the others could easily board the boat whilst carrying their packs and was cleaning the windows in the little cabin, as they had become quite cloudy and difficult to see out of.

'Ahoy, shipmates!' shouted Brillo. Tog and Brillo waved over their friends as they walked down the jetty towards the boat.

They were happy to see them both getting on so well and pleased that they were in good spirits, especially Tog, who had only just lost everything he owned, including his home the day before. 'Right then, how's it looking, Brillo?' asked Plod as he put his pack, including his sword cane and belt in the wooden trunk at the rear of the boat. Ping and Tam also placed their packs into the storage area. 'Are we good to go?'

'Yep, looks it,' confirmed Brillo. 'OK, is everyone comfortable?' They all nodded to Brillo as he leapt onto the floating wooden jetty and untied the rope from the mooring post, throwing it back onto the deck. Tog caught it and wound it neatly, placing it to the side of the deck so no one would trip on it. 'Thanks, Tog, looks like

I've found my first mate,' Brillo grinned to his friends as he pushed the boat out and jumped back on deck. Once the boat had slowly turned into position, Tog helped him raise the sails and they headed towards the mouth of the River Olden, north towards Eagles Breath. Tog stood on the deck and waved to Pip who was standing on the walkway above the boatyard, she had come to see him off, this would probably be the last time he saw his friend or the town of Olden's Moat. He had a lump in his throat as he whispered "goodbye" to his home.

They were making good time as the river was unusually empty. Being one of the main waterways in Wilstrome it was generally very busy. 'Seems a bit quiet,' remarked Plod. 'Is it usually like this, Brillo?'

'Well, this isn't a stretch of river that I've ever been on,' replied Brillo. 'But it does seem incredibly quiet, I haven't seen a single craft.' He peered through his cabin windows, carefully surveying the river, Plod's observations started to concern him somewhat. 'Tog, why is it so quiet? Surely it's not normally like this?'

'It is strange,' replied Tog. 'All the boats coming and going into Olden's Moat the last couple of weeks have been using the other waterways that flow into the town. I did wonder why this stretch of the River Olden was being avoided but didn't think much of it.' He shrugged, staring ahead into the distance, then he narrowed his eyes in thought. 'Now I think of it ... there is something that deters folk from taking this particular stretch of river ... whenever there has been a recent storm.' He put his hand to his head and scratched his brow in thought. 'I'm sorry, guys, it's lost me, I've never had much experience of boats I'm afraid. Maybe this river is just prone to obstructions from the tall trees that line the bank?'

'Hmm, maybe,' replied Brillo, looking unsure. 'The stretch heading south, back towards my home village of Clamshell Nook was blocked yesterday due to a fallen tree, but I wouldn't have thought it's any more likely to be an issue on this waterway?'

Whilst the others were discussing the unusually quiet river, Tam and Ping's interest was elsewhere, at the stern of the boat. They were peering over the rear and watching a bow wave on the surface, just a few yards from the boat. 'Wow, Ping,' said Tam. 'Do you think it's a river dolphin coming up for air?'

'I don't know,' replied Ping, excitedly. 'I hope so, they are extremely rare.' She turned back to the others, 'Hey guys, I think a dolphin is coming up to say hello!'

'Really?' said Brillo. 'They are an incredibly rare sight.' He left the cabin and followed Tog and Plod over to the rear of the boat, hoping to get a glimpse of the rare species.

'It doesn't seem to be breaking the surface?' said Plod. 'I'm surprised it's not coming up for air, that bow wave looks huge, how big do the river dolphins get?' He looked confused as he studied the massive bow wave with his companions.

'You know ...' started Tog, he seemed to suddenly remember something as he watched the bow wave. 'I've overheard fisherman in the Pike mention something about this ... oh that's it! The storm, it brings something to the surface, now what is it ... I don't think its river dolphin. Iron-heads, that's it! I remember now, the storms confuse them, and they come to the surface, confusing anything that makes a ripple in the water as prey, including boats,' he beamed triumphantly, pleased that he had remembered why the river was so quiet, then his smile quickly slipped. 'Iron-heads!' screamed Tog, putting his hands to his head and looking from the bow wave and back to his new comrades in a frantic manner.

'Iron-head!' screamed Brillo as he ran over to the mainsail and pushed the boom, so it took the wind. 'It'll ram the boat! It's going to smash the hull to pieces!'

'What can we do to help!' screamed Ping as they stared at the looming presence of the bow wave. The iron-head was hunting the boat and biding its time, waiting to attack. The Iron-head was a huge, predatory fish and this one was at least 20ft long with a gigantic, bulbous head. It was armour plated with bone on the outside, like an exoskeleton, which is said to be as strong as iron. It was also thought that they could sense the tiniest ripple or vibration in the water using their heads. They killed their prey by ramming them with this formidable weapon, tracking them until they felt ready to attack, occasionally stunning larger fish but usually killing instantly.

'Get away from the stern!' shouted Brillo to his friends as he grabbed hold of the wheel. 'Everyone in the cabin!'

As they ran towards the cabin, the iron-head struck. It wasn't with full force, it seemed to be testing its prey. A cracking, splitting sound could be heard from the rear of the boat, they staggered and nearly fell as they ran into the little cabin.

'We're taking on water!' shrieked Tam.

Plod tried to keep his composure, 'Brillo, what can

we do? We can't outrun it can we?' Brillo didn't say anything for a moment as he stared out the window, thinking.

'Nothing can outrun an iron-head,' replied Brillo.

'We need to distract it somehow,' said Plod.

'Yes, a distraction,' replied Tog. 'That might just work.' The gillsprog stood outside the cabin for a moment, staring at the bow wave. He turned back to his new friends, 'Thank you for showing me so much kindness, I've not had much of that in my life ...' He slowly turned back towards the rear of the boat and ran. He jumped high and far, diving deep into the water behind the iron-head. The fish instantly turned, sensing the vibrations in the water and shot towards Tog as he swam at incredible speed, taking the predator far away from the boat.

'Noooo!' screamed Brillo as he ran to the back of the boat, nearly plunging over the side as he grabbed the rail, kneeling on the wooden trunk.

'Brillo!' shrieked Ping as she ran over to him, worried he was going to jump in, after his new friend. They pulled Brillo back from the edge and tried to calm him.

Tam rested a hand on his shoulder, trying to console him, 'He saved us all, Brillo.'

'That he did,' added Plod, resting a paw on his leg, deeply saddened by what had just happened.

Brillo turned to the damaged hull, snapping out of the emotional state he was in, realising he had to do something before they sank. 'There's too much water!' shouted Brillo. 'We need to make it over to the bank. There's no point in continuing down the Olden anyway, not with the threat of the iron-heads.' The boat was taking on a massive amount of water, but after 20 minutes of slowly drifting towards the bank, they were finally close enough to get across without having to swim and risk an iron-head attack. They used the gangway plank and placed one edge on the roof of the cabin to get over to the bank; the boat was close to sinking. They had already thrown their packs onto the adjacent path, including the two crossbows and Plod's sword cane.

The four companions sat on the river bank, getting their breath back. They stared at the boat as it disappeared from view, as it was pulled into the dark depths of the river.

'I… don't know what to say, Brillo,' said Plod, tapping his paw on the young boy's leg. Tam and Ping looked over to them in a state of despair.

'Well … it was an old boat,' replied Brillo with a sad half-smile. 'Probably only had a couple more years at best left in her anyway. The good memories of being with my father in that boat, will always be with me, I don't need an old bit of wood to remember him by.' He took his penknife out of his pocket and turned it around in his hands as he spoke, it was obviously a gift from his late father.

As they took their time to ponder the situation, staring into the river, Plod noticed something. 'What's that,' he said, motioning out to a bow wave in the distance.

'I imagine it's another iron-head chasing its prey,' replied Ping, watching the disturbance on the surface of the water.

'Whatever it is, it appears to be coming towards us at great speed,' added Tam as he rose up and flapped his wings, hovering a few feet above the bank.

The others stood up and watched the bow wave, chasing its prey directly towards them on the river bank. 'Eh, maybe we should stand back!' said Plod. As they took a few steps back, something broke the surface and shot out of the water. Startled, they instinctively ducked, and Tam flew swiftly out the way.

'Whooaa!' shrieked Tog as he shot out of the water and disappeared, tumbling into some long grass behind the others. At that same moment, the iron-head struck the bank with so much force the ground trembled and they all fell over, with a towering wave of water splashing over them. The iron-head, clearly enraged, shook its powerful head from side to side and swam off, in search of new prey.

'Haha! Tog!' screeched Brillo in delight, getting himself up after the soaking. 'It seems there is one thing in all of Wilstrome able to outpace a hungry iron-head; a homeless gillsprog from the aqua town of Olden's Moat, who goes by the name of Tog!' They all started laughing as they made their way over to Tog, being careful not to tumble on the now slippery bank.

'Oh my!' panted the breathless gillsprog. 'I can't believe ... I made it,' he panted heavily, exhausted, but with a smile spreading across his face.

Brillo held out his hand and helped Tog to his feet, 'Unbelievable,' said Brillo, grinning. 'One out of two isn't bad, at least we got our Tog back. Unfortunately, my boat hasn't fared so well.'

'That was very courageous of you, Tog,' said Plod. 'We're all extremely impressed, without your bravery we would surely have become an easy meal for the iron-heads.'

'When you said you were a good swimmer, Tog' said Ping. 'I didn't doubt you, but I admit I wasn't expecting to see you again once you dived into the river.'

'No, nor was I expecting to see you guys again,' replied Tog, his breathing nearly back to normal.

'It seems we are on foot then from here on,' said Plod.

'Do you know the way from here, Tog?'

'Unfortunately, no,' replied Tog. 'If we continue following the river north, we should come across it at some stage though.'

'We'll have to go through that wildflower meadow,' observed Brillo. 'The tangle of bushes and weeds look way too dense up ahead to cross on foot.' They all agreed and after taking a moment to drink some water and ensure Tog had got his energy back, they entered the wildflower meadow opposite the bank.

Following the river close to the water was made impossible by the deep, wide thickets, woven with weeds and thistles. The meadow was breath-taking. An endless matt of small wildflowers was interspersed with huge giants that towered into the sky; their stems as thick as the largest trees in all of Walnut Point. Some of these giant flowers weren't just pretty to look at, they were deadly man-eaters, in fact they would eat any creature that moved and were extremely predatory. Unfortunately, some of the dangerous varieties were difficult to distinguish, if not impossible. There are those that were just huge round buds showing an open mouth containing many rows of sharp teeth. Others resembled ordinary flowers - apart from their massive size - until the centre of the flower quickly opened up to show a huge set of sharp-toothed jaws, ready to chomp and snatch its unsuspecting prey. Then they draw their catch down into the corrosive, acidic liquid that fills their cavernous stems to digest their kill.

'Everyone needs to keep their wits about them in this meadow,' said Plod, leading the group carefully through the wildflowers, walking warily on his hind legs, with his unsheathed sword cane in hand. 'You've all heard the stories, be wary of the dangerous looking flowers and even more careful of the completely innocent looking ones.' The other members of the group nodded to themselves, looking up at the imposing wildflowers in awe. Tog visibly gulped, having evaded a 20ft iron-head he didn't plan on being eaten by a flower.

It was early afternoon and they had spent a couple of hours carefully treading their way through the meadow. The man-eaters would only respond to touch, so it was important not to brush past the millions of sensitive hairs, which covered their stems.

'Wow imagine getting caught by that!' said Brillo, looking up at a particularly dangerous looking flower. It just looked like a massive, round bud on a huge stem. The top of the bud was covered in spikes and a cavernous, circular mouth faced their direction and rows of razor-sharp teeth tapered deep into its mouth. It seemed to rotate continually in a mechanical fashion, each row rotating in opposite directions.

As Tog looked up at what had taken Brillo's attention, he instinctively took a step back in horror, losing his footing and stumbling backwards into a thick flower stem. 'Ahhhrggg!' he screeched, quickly getting to his feet and looking up at the flower, 'Phew, I think you're a safe one, that was close.'

'You OK, Tog,' asked Tam as he and Ping quickly went to Tog's aid.

'Yeah, I was just taken by surprise when I looked at that flower Brillo was talking about,' replied Tog.

As he spoke, the stem he had just rolled into arched over and two gigantic claws - much like a crab's claws – seemed to unfold themselves from the centre of the flower. Enormous, bright blue petals framed the snapping pincers, they watched in horror as it went towards Plod and Brillo, who were up ahead and totally oblivious to the situation behind them.

They turned when they heard the groaning, creaking sound of the gigantic stem arching towards them. 'Plod!' screamed Tog. 'Brillo! Run!'

They turned at the last minute, caught off guard and too late to avoid the clutches of the flower's claws. 'Plod!' screamed Brillo. 'Help!' The flower had snatched up both Plod and Brillo. It had Brillo by his shirt and Plod by his leather sword belt. The weasel was still clutching his sword cane and instinctively swung it with all his might at the claw holding his friend. The ultra-sharp blade cut through the claw arm, causing an explosion of strange blue mist to shoot briefly out of the severed claw arm in a powerful plume. Startled, Plod dropped his cane, which fell to the ground and landed blade-end down, like a stake in the earth.

'Ahhhrggh!' screamed Plod. 'My cane!'

Tog ran towards them with Tam and Ping close behind. 'What can we do!' shrieked Tog. 'Tam! Ping! What do we do!' Tog was panicking, running around, looking up at his friends high above. When he saw Plod slice through the claw arm, he held out his arms in the hope to break Brillo's fall.

'He's too high!' screeched Tam, flying at maximum speed towards the young boy, who was hurtling towards the ground. He knew that the fall was too high for Tog to catch him, they would both end up with catastrophic injuries, or worse.

'Ahhhrrggg! Noooo!' screamed Brillo as he fell.

Tam swooped in and clutched onto Brillo's shirt, he managed to hold him for a few seconds and get him closer to the ground before he was no longer able to hold his weight and his shirt ripped. Fortunately, he'd slowed his fall and brought him close enough to the ground so that Tog was able to attempt to break his fall. 'Whoooaaaa!' screamed Tog as he held out his hands. 'Brillo!' He fell into Togs arms and they both stumbled and rolled across the ground, which seemed to sufficiently break his fall as they both got away with minor bruises.

'Plod!' screamed Ping. 'I'm coming!' The others turned and watched Ping. The focus had now turned to their companion, hanging helplessly from the flowers claw. Tog and Brillo were left winded from the fall but were now standing. They held onto one another, as they watched Ping run up the towering flower stem.

The stem was at an extremely steep angle, but Ping was agile, her sharp claws sinking into the stem and giving her a solid grip. As she sprinted towards the flower, she jumped and sunk her teeth into the claw arm, swinging around and letting go as she reached her highest point. She flew through the air and slid skilfully back down the stem. Blue liquid began to seep out of the flower's wounded claw arm, and it let go of Plod causing him to plummet towards the ground. Tam once again flapped his wings with purpose and shot towards his friend. Fortunately, Plod was a lot lighter than Brillo and his leather belt a lot stronger than Brillo's old shirt. Tam clutched onto his sword belt and just about managed to hold on as they dropped towards the ground. It wasn't the smoothest landing and they both stumbled as they hit the earth below, but fortunately, they were uninjured.

The flower retracted its wounded claw and the remaining claw arm, which had been severed from Plod's attack. Miraculously, it went back to its fully upright position, as if nothing had ever happened.

'Woohoo!' shouted Brillo, punching the air. 'I can't believe it, Plod, we're actually in one piece.'

'Haha!' replied Plod, tapping Brillo on the leg with his paw. 'Well done everyone, great work,' he said, still breathless as he winked at Ping, knowing without her, he would have become the flowers next meal. She returned his gesture with a pleased grin. 'And to add to my previous comments regarding the potential danger of those giant wildflowers, that is why we don't go near any of the stems.' He started chuckling, euphoric that it had been a positive outcome. The others couldn't help but laugh, even though they knew how close they had just come to a tragic end.

Plod walked over to his sword cane and tugged it from the earth. He wiped off the blade, which was smeared with dirt and the strange blue liquid from the flower and then swooshed it from side to side a couple of times. 'Let's get out of here, guys,' said Brillo. 'I think I would like to bring our stroll through the wildflower meadow to an end.' The others strongly agreed with Brillo's assessment and they continued their journey, following Plod who once again took the lead. Although this time, they stayed close and looked straight ahead, whilst taking care with their footing.

Chapter 7

It had been a long and eventful day and the sun was now starting to set. It had taken a few hours to leave the dangers of the wildflower meadow behind and another hour's trek before the large town of Eagles Breath came into view, framed by the sun, which was a ghostly burnt orange as it rippled, descending behind the mountains in the distance.

'Let's find somewhere to eat and get a room for the night, guys,' said Plod. The others nodded in agreement, feeling tired and in need of a drink and a decent meal. They approached a large stone arch with a muscular guard standing on either side. They each carried a long polearm with savage-looking axe heads, and they were protected by tall shields. Their leather armour looked robust and well made. They nodded to the group as they headed through the archway. The town was situated on the bank of the River Olden and had two entrances, a stone archway on the south side of the town, which they had just entered and one at the north end, where you would come out next to the river, headed north. The whole town was protected by a 20ft high stone wall, which connected the north and south archways. A long wooden jetty ran the length of the town on the river side and was set about ten yards from the stone wall. If you moored up here, you would still need to make your way around to one of the arches and go past the guards to enter the town.

'Wow,' remarked Tam as they approached the centre of the town. 'Look at that statue!'

'Yep, it's always an impressive sight' replied Plod, acknowledging the dramatic statue as the group came to a stop and admired it whilst there was still just enough light. As well as being known for its many Inns and the adventurer's guilds, Eagles Breath also had a magnificent eagle statue in the centre of town. It was crafted entirely out of bronze and was seen as a show of strength in a town known for its warriors, hunters and fearless adventurers.

Not far from the eagle statue, was the place that Tog had mentioned the day before, 'That building over there is the Guild & Inn,' stated Tog. 'We should get something to eat and drink and take a well needed rest.' They all agreed, Tog and Brillo rubbed their cuts and bruises as they all walked over to the inn. They had fared the worst from the group's ordeal due to Brillo's fall.

It was fairly quiet inside the inn. A couple of barmen were in conversation behind the bar and a dwarf was sitting in front of them, drinking from a large tankard. His hammer, which looked impossibly heavy when compared to his size, was leant up against the bar. A large, square fire pit was set in the centre of the inn and was full of glowing orange embers, which gave off a welcoming warmth. A few folk sat around tables, drinking and playing cards but it wasn't busy. Tog chose a large rectangular table beside the fire pit. 'What do you think?' asked Tog.

'Perfect,' replied Ping as they all took a seat, placing

their packs and Plod's sword cane in a pile next to them. They let out relieved sighs of exhaustion as they finally got to sit down. They just sat grinning at one another for a moment, pleased they had survived the day and were still all somehow together at the end of it.

'Hello travellers,' said a tall, striking, red-haired woman in a welcoming voice.

They suddenly turned to face her, having not seen her approach as they were all still grinning, taking in the events of the day. 'Hello there,' replied Plod.

'Well, this is an interesting group,' said the woman. 'I seldom see a small horn away from their wood, and a ... two-footed scritch?' Tam gave his usual pleased bow with a smile and she smiled back in return, surprised to see such a rare creature at the inn. 'My name is Tabitha, and this here is my guild and inn, I'm the guildmaster. You all look like you could do with a good feed and a tankard of strome mead.' They all nodded and grinned eagerly. 'I'll also bring something out to clean up those cuts.' She motioned to Tog and Brillo before walking over to the bar staff and having a quick word before going through a door to the side.

A few minutes later she returned with a bowl of water and a flannel, 'Looks like you guys have been on quite an adventure,' she said as she cleaned up Tog and Brillo's cuts. 'You're in Eagles Breath, in the Guild & Inn, come on out with it, what have you been up to?' she said grinning at the group, eager to hear their tale.

They explained the journey from Olden's Moat, including the altercation with an iron-head, which led them into the wildflower meadow and the battle for their lives with a ferocious, giant wildflower. 'And that's pretty much our journey to Eagles Breath,' finished Plod.

'Not quite as we had planned but at least we all made it here in one piece.' They all chuckled, including Tabitha.

'Wow,' she replied. 'That's quite a day you've had, I'm genuinely impressed. You're obviously a capable band, you can call me Tabs.' Tabs was tall and slender with long, flame red hair flowing down to her waist, she wore a classic, round brimmed hunters' hat and a brown leather jacket, a black leather skirt met the top of a sturdy looking set of dark green knee-high boots. She was armed with a short sword, which hung on a belt to her side and a long bow, which was attached to a quiver of arrows on her back.

'Nice to meet you, Tabs,' said Brillo. 'Thanks for cleaning up our cuts.' Tog nodded and thanked her.

'If you all want to get cleaned up, we have rooms,' said Tabs.

'That would be fantastic, Tabs,' replied Plod. 'Yes please.'

'No problem,' replied Tabs. 'I have a three bed and a two-bed available, just pay three gold coin for the three bed and they're both yours for the night.'

'That's most kind of you,' replied Tam. At that point, the drinks arrived at the table, including Brillo's small tankard. Five large plates of food were set down in front of them, which consisted of a mountain of sliced meat and a mixture of steaming vegetables.

'This looks incredible, Tabs,' said Ping. 'Thank you.' Tabs smiled at the group as they eagerly got started on their meals and drinks.

'Would you care to have a drink with us, Tabs?' asked Plod.

'I would love to,' replied Tabs as she pulled up a chair. 'It's been a long day.'

After the group had finished their food and everyone had ordered more drinks, Tabs was curious to learn more about this intriguing group and the quest they had undertaken. 'So, come on, guys, you must be on a quest of some sort, I should know, after all, I am a hunter who owns an adventurer's guild and inn. Enlighten me, what's the quest?' Plod looked from Tabs to the group with a more serious expression, unsure of what he should offer in response. Tabs narrowed her eyes slightly, now looking more serious. 'You know,' she started as she leant into the group, looking around and keeping her voice hushed. 'There has been some anxious chatter around town recently, about, you know … the monster in the mountains. Apparently, its stirring again, some say there have been sightings and a party is being put together once more, on the order of town and village leaders?'

They look to one another in silence for a moment. 'Can you keep a secret Tabs?' asked Plod in a serious tone.

'Yes, of course,' replied Tabs, sincere in her response.

'We are the hunting party,' confirmed Plod. 'I'm the weasel who fought the monster three years ago and I wouldn't be alive now, if it weren't for my good friend here, Tam. I was the only surviving member of that particular band.'

'Ha!' said Tabs, not raising her voice too loud. 'I thought it could be you, it's a pleasure to meet you, in fact it's a pleasure to meet all of you, you're on a grave quest indeed.' She now lowered her gaze, aware that this could be one of the last meals these brave souls would enjoy.

'We're actually looking for a couple more members to join our party, before we track the beast in the mountains and attempt to defeat it once and for all.' said Plod, holding Tab's gaze. 'We are looking for two more that are skilled with blade and bow.'

She sat for a moment in silence before responding, 'You're a hunting party, I'm a hunter, one of the most respected in all of Eagles Breath.' After a few more moments, she held out a hand.

Plod put a paw on her hand, then the others quickly followed. 'Looks like our little hunting party has just increased by one,' grinned Plod. The others also exchanged smiles with Tabs, and they all took a hearty swig from their drinks.

'So, Plod,' said Brillo. 'Were just looking for one more to join our group then?'

'Yes, another hunter or warrior,' replied Plod, taking a sip from his strome mead.

'Maybe I can help you with that, guys,' said Tabs, she had the others attention, they nodded for her to continue through sips of their beers. 'I know of a warrior dwarf who may be happy to help us. He's quite a recluse and lives in the isolated Riftbrook area of Wilstrome, in a cave behind one of its many waterfalls. He goes by the name of Makledar. I've fought alongside him many times. Most folk think he's a bad-tempered loner but they're wrong, he just prefers his own company. I would trust him with my life, if there is a quest that needs completing – especially one as crucial as this – he's our, eh … dwarf.'

'Sounds good to me,' replied Tam. 'What do you think, Plod?'

'Yes,' agreed Plod. 'If everyone approves, I think we should go with Tab's suggestion. If he's good enough for a guildmaster then we would be foolish to turn this lead down.' The rest of the group agreed that this would be the best way to proceed. Turning this suggestion down would have meant finding another member for their band, who was not tried and tested.

'How do we get to the Riftbrook area from here?' asked Tog. 'I'm not familiar with the area, will this journey take us further away from the Loftpeak mountains?'

'No, in fact it's ideal, Tog,' replied Plod. 'Riftbrook lies between us, here in Eagles Breath and our destination, in the Loftpeak mountains.'

'Yes, that's quite right, Plod,' added Tabs. 'The only obstacle for us reaching Riftbrook are the sheer cliffs that surround it. They are full of cave and tunnel systems, but fortunately, I can guide us into the area.' She grinned at her new companions.

'Great, that's agreed then,' confirmed Plod. 'We head for Riftbrook at first light.' It was getting late when they finished their last round of beers. Tabs bid farewell to her new party and said she would be waiting for them in the bar area by first light. Tog and Brillo took the two bed and the others headed for the three-bed room. Thoroughly exhausted from the long, eventful day, they had no problem falling to sleep.

At first light the group made their way down to the bar area, where Tabs sat by the large fire pit, warming her hands in the cold morning air. She smiled at her comrades as they walked over and placed their packs on the floor. 'Good night's rest?' asked Tabs as she continued to warm her hands.

'Yes, thanks,' replied Tam. 'Very comfortable, I feel

refreshed and ready for our trek to Riftbrook.'

'Well, before we leave, I've got breakfast coming out for us in minute. We don't want to leave on an empty stomach as it will take a good day's trek to get to Makledar's home.' They all sat around the same table as the night before, warming themselves beside the fire pit. Moments later, the breakfast arrived and consisted of plates piled high with crusty rolls, some filled with rift elk meat and others with fried eggs. A couple of separate plates had a range of mixed, fresh fruits and a large jug of water was set on the table with six tankards.

'Tabs, do you have the items for me that we arranged last night?' asked Plod, looking over to Tabs as he took a bite out of a meat filled roll. The others looked at each other slightly confused.

'Ahh yes, I do, one minute, Plod.' Tabs gave Plod a knowing wink as she briefly left the bar area, into a back room and returned with some items, which appeared to be clothes and placed them in the centre of the table.

'Fantastic, thank you, Tabs,' said Plod, the others still looking none the wiser. 'Last night, when everyone else went up to the rooms, I went to find Tabs and asked her if she could acquire a few items for me.' He turned to Tog and Brillo who were sitting together on one side of the table. 'These are for you two, new clothes, you have both more than earnt them.' Brillo and Tog looked at each other with raised eyebrows, looking stunned and put down their rolls. 'As we head further north it will start to get cold, very cold in fact, especially when we head deep into the Loftpeak mountains, the peaks are covered in snow and the environment is harsh. Brillo, I'm sure you will be happy to lose that shirt, it's badly ripped anyway due to yesterday's giant wildflower experience.' They all smiled at one another. 'And I'm sure you will be happy to get out of those shorts, especially as the weather gets bitterly cold.' He handed Brillo his new clothes. 'Tog, going by your little swim with the iron-head yesterday in the icy depths of the River Olden.' They all chuckled. 'I imagine you don't particularly feel the cold, but your clothes were not in the best shape to start with and the impromptu swim, along with the wildflower attack, has not done them any favours.' He handed Tog his new clothes. The gifts were gratefully received. They looked as though they were holding back tears, overcome with emotion from this gesture by their kind new friend.

'I ... don't know what to say,' said Brillo, his voice breaking slightly. 'I can't remember the last time I had new clothes, for that matter I don't think I have ever had "new" clothes as they were always second hand.' Brillo looked through his new clothing, Tabs had organised a full hunter's outfit for him. As well as a warm looking shirt and long johns, he also had a rugged pair of light brown trousers and a tough, durable, light brown leather jacket, with a hood sewn in, which had a fur-lined hood. The outfit was complete with a strong, hard-wearing pair of leather, fur-lined boots.

Tog had been given a new short sleeved shirt and some black trousers to replace his current, ravaged clothing. 'Thank you so much for this,' said Tog with a tear in his eye. 'I've not had many friends in my life, espe-cially ones that would do something like this for me ... I will never forget this kindness.'

'You two should change into your new clothes,' said Tam, grinning, pleased to see his two new friends so happy.

'Yep,' added Ping as she finished her breakfast, smiling at her two companions. 'Sounds like we have a long day's trek ahead of us.'

'Ok,' said Plod. 'We'll check on the provisions and get our packs strapped on, ready for the trip whilst you both get ready.' Brillo and Tog eagerly left the room with their new clothes. Tabs had told them to use a little room, which was just behind the bar to get changed.

Once finished, they made their way back over to the rest of the group. 'Perfect,' remarked Plod, pleased that his friends were clearly so happy with their well-earned gifts, the others nodding in agreement. 'I think that's it then, let's head for Riftbrook, Tabs, you take the lead.'

'OK,' nodded Tabs. 'Before we leave, I've packed some extra provisions and equipment, Brillo, Tog, would you mind taking these extra packs.' They nodded and picked up the leather rucksacks as she put her bow and quiver of arrows in place on her back. The others secured their own packs. Tabs had replenished their provisions and water flasks and Plod secured his sword cane in place. The seized thief-kind crossbows were placed in Brillo and Togs packs. Tabs had passed on her responsibilities at the Guild & Inn to another senior guild member for the duration of the quest. She didn't explain the details, nor did she indicate when, or if, she would return. They were all set and ready to leave for Riftbrook and hopefully, would soon recruit the seventh and final member of their party, the warrior dwarf, Makledar.

The band of six left the safety of Eagle Breath's tall stone walls and headed out of the town's northern arch and travelled north east, in the direction of the Loftpeak mountains and their next destination, Riftbrook. The journey between Eagles Breath and Riftbrook was entirely on foot, through an enormous forest of tall pine trees. The ground was covered in a blanket of moss in every shade of green, it covered the many large rocks and boulders strewn throughout the forest, and the ancient pines looked as though they are being slowly enveloped and taken over by the green moss. The only living things that seemed to have evaded the capture of the moss, are the many toadstools and fungi that grow at all angles out of the ground and off the rocks and trees, triumphantly piercing the green carpet. It's eerily quiet in the forest as the morning sun slowly disperses a lingering fog.

By midday, the group had made good progress through the pine forest with Tabs leading the band. She knew the forest well and had made the trip to her old friend, Makledar, many times to seek his assistance on difficult quests. 'Now the fog has gone,' started Tabs. 'You should just be able to make out the tall cliffs in the distance, through the pines.' A steep hill led up to the base of the cliffs which encircled Riftbrook.

'So, Tabs,' said Brillo, slightly out of breath as he got used to the weight of his new clothing and the rucksack. 'You know the network of caves and tunnels well then, that run through these cliffs?'

'Oh, I'm sure Tabs knows them like the back of her hand, Brillo?' added Tog, confidently.

'No not at all.' replied Tabs.

'See, I told you … pardon, what was that again, Tabs?' asked Tog looking suddenly confused.

The others came to an abrupt stop, as Tabs continued walking until she realised and turned around to face her comrades.

'Tabs, I thought you knew your way through the tunnels?' queried Plod.

'I never actually said we were to go through the cliffs, via the caves and tunnels,' said Tabs with a wry smile. 'We're going over the top. Brillo, Tog, did you check the packs I gave you?' They shook their heads, looking dumbfounded at this revelation as they opened their packs.

'Oh,' said Brillo as he and Tog opened their rucksacks. 'I see ... it appears I have a strong coil of rope in my pack amongst the provisions.'

'Same here ...' added Tog. They both suddenly went pale, the idea of scaling the cliffs did not sit well with them.'

Plod, Tam and Ping started to snigger, not having any issues with heights at all. 'Come on now guys,' said Plod, turning to his friends whilst trying to compose himself. 'Brillo, you've shown great bravery and ability, that's why you're here. Tog, you've more than proved yourself already. Do neither of you have any experience of heights at all?'

'Well,' started Brillo. 'The experience I have is confined more to water level.' He narrowed his eyes in the direction of Plod and starting to look slightly annoyed. He shot glances between Tabs and the others, not looking very impressed. 'Primarily the River Olden, Plod, I've already had to endure being picked up by a man-eating wildflower and plummeting to the ground, only narrowly escaping serious injury or worse!'

Tog looked equally unimpressed, glancing at the others with a displeased expression. 'Other than the stilt houses of Olden's Moat, Plod, my comfort level is also on the River Olden!' The others tried to stifle their sniggering, not wanting to laugh at their friends' expense.

'Look guys,' said Ping. 'It's going to be fine; Tabs knows this route well.'

'Well, that's easy for you to say, Ping' said Brillo, mumbling under his breath. 'You're happy sprinting up the side of giant wildflower stems, I don't think you've got anything to worry about.'

'Come on now,' added Tam with a gentle smile, trying to calm his two friends. 'There's nothing to worry about, we're all going over the cliffs as a team and we'll help one another.'

'Hmmph, OK,' said Tog, also now mumbling under his breath. 'If I had wings, I don't think I would be too troubled either.'

Tabs walked up to them both and put a hand on each of their shoulders. She was trying to think of something positive and constructive to say but burst out laughing. She couldn't help but laugh at the image of their faces when they saw the ropes and their mumbling responses to the others. They both stared at her for a moment and then looked at each other and burst out laughing along with the rest of the party.

'OK, OK, maybe we overacted slightly,' said Brillo as they calmed down. Tog also agreed, they both seemed to be blushing from their knee-jerk reactions.

'Come on then,' said Plod once everyone had settled down. 'The cliffs are not far ahead, let's try and scale them and make contact with Makledar before sundown.' They all agreed with this, even Brillo and Tog, they didn't want to attempt scaling the cliffs at nightfall, they already thought it was bad enough in daylight.

∞∞∞

After a 20-minute hike up the hill, they had reached the base of the sheer, moss covered cliffs on the border of the pine forest. The section which Tabs had chosen was noticeably lower than the surrounding cliffs as a lot of rock had fallen away, leaving a rocky slope that would make the final quarter of the climb to the summit much easier. The easiest part of the climb, up to the rock slope, was still 60ft and Brillo and Tog both gulped as they stared up, towards the clifftop.

'OK, try not to worry you two,' said Tabs as she pulled out the ropes from their packs. 'I'm going to free climb up to the summit and secure one of the ropes over this side, and then secure the second one in place and drop over the other side, when I reach the top.' Brillo and Tog nervously glanced at one another.

'Cliff skimmers,' said Plod, standing on his hind legs and putting a paw to his brow, trying not to stare into the sun as he squinted at the summit.

'Yes, I didn't really want to draw anyone's attention to those,' replied Tabs, shooting Plod a glance and gesturing to Brillo and Tog. Plod scrunched his face up and mouthed "sorry". 'Yes, the cliff skimmers are often here, we just need to scale the cliff and get over the other side before sundown.'

'Eh, Tabs,' said Tog. 'What are cliff skimmers? Are they going to cause us a problem?' He Looked to Brillo as he asked the question, his friend had a blank expression and shrugged.

'I take it neither of you have come across the skimmers before?' asked Tabs as she checked the climbing ropes. They looked to one another and shook their heads. 'The cliff skimmers are large, jet black, raven-like birds, strikingly similar to ravens in fact. The noticeable differences being that they are about three times the size. Their beaks are also much longer, which can reach lengths of over ten inches and as well as an extremely sharp point, the top and bottom of the bill has a razor-sharp edge, much like a double-edged knife blade.' Both Brillo and Tog suddenly looked pale and wore horrified expressions. 'They use this for spearing prey in the air, such as the other smaller clifftop species that can be found hovering over the summit. They don't hunt until low light though; their vision is exceptional and being jet black means they can pick off their prey with stealth when it starts to get dark. We wouldn't be their typical target as we are not their usual prey. We just don't want to be scaling the cliffs when they are in a hunting frenzy ... you wouldn't want to be in the way of their next kill.'

Brillo and Tog just stared at Tabs in shock, the idea of climbing the cliff was unsettling enough, but now images of massive, knife-beaked ravens flying towards them entered their thoughts. 'Come on, guys,' said Plod as he walked over to them with Tam and Ping, snapping them out of their troubling thoughts. 'As Tabs mentioned, cliff skimmers don't hunt in the day, and they won't even descend until low light when they come down to hunt.'

'I keep hearing the word "hunt",' replied Brillo. 'It's not really what I wanted to hear just before my first attempt at scaling a cliff.' They both looked miserable again.

'Let's just get this over and done with,' added Tam, as he placed a hand on each of their shoulders to help calm them down.

'Yes,' added Ping. 'And anyway, this is really the least of our worries really, notwithstanding our quest to defeat the Skinkadink, who's lair is in the mountains ...' They weren't sure if this comment from Ping had helped or just made things worse, but they had come this far and weren't going to stop now. The only way forward was up and over the cliff.

'OK, Tam,' said Tabs. 'Could you do me a favour and take this other rope up to the summit please? I'll take the other over my shoulder.

'Yes, of course, Tabs,' replied Tam as his companion handed him the rope.

'It won't take me long,' said Tabs as she approached the base of the cliff and rubbed her hands together, looking up at the peak. Tam flew up to the top so he could take the other rope up to the summit. Tabs started her ascent, expertly finding the foot and hand holds she needed to scale the cliff face at dizzying speed. The others looked to one another, raising their eyebrows, astounded at the hunter's display. She reached the top in no more than five minutes and waved down to her friends at the base. She set about tying her rope around a large, pointed section of rock which jutted out of the cliff summit, making sure it was secure. 'OK!' shouted Tabs as she peered over the edge. 'I'm going to throw down the rope! It may be best if Brillo and Tog go first!'

'Yes! no problem!' shouted Ping as the rope came hurtling down and whipped against the cliff face.

'Who's first then?' asked Plod, looking from Brillo to Tog.

'I'll go,' replied Brillo, grudgingly. Tog stepped aside, happy to observe his friend's attempt. 'Let's just get this out of the way as quick as possible.' Plod showed him what to do. Tam flew right next to him for support and to aid him if he slipped. To his surprise, he was making short work of the cliff face. 'Tog!' shouted Brillo as he climbed. 'This isn't so bad you know!' He was clearly starting to enjoy his first rock climbing experience and it was not long before he was scaling the sloped section that led to the top. Tog looked on with an uneasy smile. 'I did it!' he shouted, jumping around with joy on the top of the cliff. Tabs was impressed and grinned as she gave him a high five.

'Tog! You're up next!' shouted Tabs.

Tog hesitantly approached the rope. 'OK! Here I come!' he shouted, trying to sound as confident as possible. Tam did the same for Tog and kept him calm and reassured. 'Ha! You're right, Brillo, this isn't too bad!' He also surprised himself and made quick work of the climb. Once at the summit he high fived Brillo and Tabs, pleased with his effort.

Once Brillo and Tog were safely at the top, Tam flew up to them and waited for Plod and Ping. Just before they began to make their ascent, thick grey clouds blocked out the sun and everything went very dim as the light level suddenly dropped. 'Guys!' shouted Tabs. 'Let's make quick work of this! Cliff skimmers!' The low light had drawn the cliff skimmers nearer to the clifftop as they began to search for prey.

'Quick, go Ping, go!' shouted Plod. Ping jumped to the rope and bolted up to the summit with blistering speed. As soon as she had made it to the summit, Plod pounced towards the rope and began to ascend, also at a near impossible speed. Just as he was sprinting up the final sloped section of the cliff face, a skimmer appeared from nowhere and brushed past his head, nearly spearing him in the process. 'Ahhhrggh!' screamed Plod, stumbling but just about holding on to the rope. He turned his head, the bird was heading directly for him again, it was only a few feet away, he had no time and braced himself.

Inches before Plod was impaled by the skimmer, an arrow smashed into its side with great force, sending it tumbling down the cliff face and striking the ground with a thud. 'Quick, Plod!' shouted Tabs, she was poised with bow in hand and drew another arrow from her quiver, guarding his final ascent up the cliff. 'Everyone against the rock and keep low!' she shouted. They all dived towards the rock, which Tabs had used to attach the rope.

'I thought the cliff skimmers wouldn't attack us on purpose!' shouted Brillo.

'It's not impossible!' shouted Tabs, as the skimmers shot past, inches above the rock outcrop. 'They're not usually so predatory, they hunt what they need to survive, something must have spooked them to be willing to attack anything!'

Plod peered around the side of the rock and could just make out the gloomy outline of their destination, Loftpeak, he wondered if they sensed the monster in the mountains. He drew his sword cane from its sheath. 'Brillo, Tog!' he shouted. 'Get the crossbows from your packs! I know you only have one bolt each but it's all we have!' They nodded and quickly grabbed them from their packs. They drew their crossbow strings and reloaded the bolts, as they had decocked the bows and removed the bolts before leaving for Riftbrook.

'How far is it to the edge of the summit, Tabs!' shouted Ping, as the aggressive cawing from the skimmers overhead grew louder.

'We could sprint it in a few minutes!' replied Tabs. 'This is why I go over the top. The cliff is so wide, and the tunnels are like a maze. The cliffs on the pine forest side have a habit of collapsing, the moss from the forest has spread within the tunnels and it has slowly weakened the rock over the years,' she explained.

'I don't know, Tabs!' screamed Tog as a cawing skimmer hit the top of the rock and bounced off. 'I think I would have taken my chances right now!'

'We need to do something, fast!' shouted Tam, his usual calm composure slipping somewhat as the skimmers got ever closer.

'OK, we're going to sprint to the opposite edge of the clifftop ... and jump!' replied Tabs.

'What do you mean, jump!' shrieked Brillo.

'On the other side of this cliff is a large pool of water!' replied Tabs. 'Makledar's waterfall flows into this over a large rock outcrop on the opposite side of the pool!'

'So, you've jumped into this pool from the clifftop before, Tabs!' queried Tog, frantically.

'... No, I've always climbed down the other side ... but I've swam in it before, it's very deep, I'm sure we will be fine!' she looked to her comrades with an uncertain grin.

'This is the only plan we have!' shouted Plod. 'And we can't stay here much longer, on the count of three we run for the edge and jump out as far as we can!' The others agreed, grimacing as the wailing skimmers continued to clatter off the rock, this was their only plan. 'Brillo, Tog! Have those crossbows at the ready, use them if you need to!' They responded with agitated nods, their fingers going pale as they gripped their bows tightly. 'Ready! One ... two ... three!'

They bolted from their positions, tight against the rock. Plod led the group with Tabs close behind, three skimmers flew straight at them. Tabs shot down the one in the middle, the arrow hit it with such force that at jolted backwards, tumbling across the ground. Plod jumped and thrusted the blade into one of the skimmers. Then in one lightning-fast movement, whilst still in the air, he withdrew the blade and slashed the cane backwards, cutting down another. They were only a minute now from the cliff edge. As Tabs went to draw another arrow, a huge skimmer was already upon her. Brillo and Tog instinctively raised their crossbows and fired, both finding their mark, the large skimmer let out a blood-curdling wail is it plummeted down and slid across the ground. Tabs turned her head and nodded her thanks to them, now seconds from the edge of the cliff face. 'Jump!' screamed Tabs.

They all leapt off the edge of the cliff, arms and legs flailing in the air. Tam flew over the edge at speed and came to a skidding stop on the bank of the pool. The others plunged into the pool, soaking Tam as they hit the water. 'Whoo-hoo!' shouted Brillo as he came to the surface, spitting out water.

'Haha! We did it!' shrieked Tog in delight.

'Yes! Well done Tabs, your plan worked!' spluttered Plod. 'Let's get out of the water and dry off our packs.' They swam over to the side and pulled themselves out of the perfectly clear water that glinted shades of green and blue. The large pool sat a few yards from the base of the cliff face and a waterfall thundered into the water on the other side, cascading over a massive rock formation, which was surrounded by fir trees. A stream snaked off down a hill in between the abundant firs, taking water away from the pool.

'It looks like it's about to rain,' remarked Tabs as she held out her hands and looked up to the sky.

'So much for drying off our packs,' added Ping.

'How far is your friend's place, Tabs?' asked Tam. 'I know you said he lives in a cave behind a waterfall.'

'Look no further, Mr Scritch!' boomed a deep voice, coming from the direction of a dwarf, peering around the side of the waterfall, which plunged into the pool. 'Haha! Tabs! Don't tell me you just jumped into the pool! I take it whatever quest you're on is not providing you with enough excitement, Haha! Quick, come on in, I think a storm is brewing!'

Chapter 8

A s Makledar ushered them into his cave it started to rain heavily, they all grabbed their packs and ran for cover. His cave was directly behind the waterfall, with a gap of a couple of feet on either side, which meant they could get into his cave without getting anymore wet. The rapids overhead made a constant rumbling sound as the river shot over the rocks and crashed into the pool below. 'Welcome, Tabs,' boomed the dwarf when they were all inside and safe from the torrential rain that had begun to fall. They embraced each other briefly and gave each other some painfully hard sounding slaps on the back. 'You must be on an interesting quest,' he said as he eyed her travelling companions carefully, squinting one eye as he scrutinised them. 'I dare say I've never seen a two-footed scritch, a young lad, a gillsprog, a eh ... yes, a cress mite - a small horn, far from her wood, and a weasel, who appears to be carrying a rarely seen weapon, a sword cane of some description.' He contemplated the group for a moment. 'Haha!' he boomed once again, taking the others slightly off-guard, except Tabs who stood next to her old friend and smiled. 'What an interesting band! Tabs, what are you up to? Come, over by the fire, dry off your packs and have a seat, I'll get us all a large tankard of strome mead each and you can tell me what's going on here.' He let out a deep chuckle as he approached a solid table, which was carved out of rock. It had a flat surface and barrels of strome mead sat on top with various tankards of all shapes and sizes scattered about on its surface. 'I always make sure to acquire a few barrels of strome mead from time to time, for eh ... special occasions,' he said as he topped up his already half full tankard of beer. He filled a range of tankards, varying in size, shape and material and handed them out to his visitors, who were now sat around the fire pit in the middle of the cave, warming their hands.

The home Makledar had made for himself in the cave was a simple one, but functional. A large fire pit was positioned in the centre with thick fur rugs encircling it. As well as his strome mead table, another slab of rock, on the other side of the fire pit, had a flat top carved into it and served as his bed. A warm looking bedroll made of a thick animal skin lined with fur lay on top. A long table had been carved into the rock at the back of the cave, which ran its full width. Jugs of water, bowls, a couple of candle lanterns that were flickering away and various items including armour and weapons were strewn across it, including a gigantic, fearsome looking hammer which rested against it. 'We are in need of your help, Mak,' said Tabs, taking a swig of her beer. 'Our quest is difficult, and chance of success is slim.'

'Ha!' replied Mak. 'Well, I knew that much already, Tabs, you wouldn't be here if it was going to be easy. This sounds like my sort of quest, please, continue.' He leant forward, now taking serious interest as shadows from the fire danced across his face.

'Let me introduce you to my friends here,' replied

Tabs. 'It may be easier if they explain.'

They all went around in turn and held up their tankards, thanking Mak whilst introducing themselves. Plod, with interjections from the others explained the reason for their quest and everything that had happened so far, including when Plod and Tam first set out from the village of Walnut Point, right up to throwing themselves off the cliff edge and into his pool. 'And that is why we find ourselves in your cave, seeking your help, sir,' said Plod as he finished the explanation. It was now dark outside and getting late and the rain was still hammering down.

'Well, well, well, quite incredible,' started Mak. 'It's a pleasure to meet you, Plod, I've heard many a tale of your perilous battle with the monster in the mountains.' He held Plod's gaze for a moment and nodded slowly, humbled to be in the weasel's presence. 'You said that you and Tam come from the village of walnut point, does an old dwarf still live there, goes by the name of Frilldar, always loved a pipe?'

'Yes,' added Tam, happily. 'Plod and I are very good friends with him, he's the village elder and leader of Walnut Point.'

'Well strike me down where I stand!' replied Mak, his eyes widening at this news. 'Old Frilldar is still alive! Well at least you've brought me some good news.'

'What do you say, Makledar, sir?' added Brillo, hoping the dwarf would join their band. 'Will you help us on our quest?' They turned from Brillo and looked to Mak, waiting on his answer.

'Well, young Brillo, lad, I was considering retirement,' replied Mak. 'This is a dangerous quest indeed, as you say, chance of a successful outcome is slim.' He lowered his gaze and took a few more deep swigs of his beer as he mulled over his thoughts. His visitors looked to one another, concerned that their close encounter with the skimmers had been in vain. 'Ha! Nearly had you there didn't I!' roared the dwarf, slapping his knee. 'Of course I will, lad! And please, you can all call me Mak. I've been itching to swing my trusty hammer again and there is nothing more I would like to swing it at, than that foul beast! Haha!' The others looked to each other with wry grins, pleased that Mak was joining their party. 'It's getting late, why don't we all get a good night's sleep and discuss the plan in the morning. I'm afraid I can't offer you anything more than the rugs in front of my fire, but I'll throw on a few more logs to keep you warm.' He walked over to a pile of cut logs stacked next to his strome mead table and threw a couple of them into the fire pit.

'That's fine by us,' replied Tabs. She looked through the gap between the cave entrance and the waterfall and it was still raining hard. She was just happy to be dry and able to keep warm next to Mak's fire. The others thanked Mak, and Tog let out a yawn which spread throughout the group. They got as comfortable as they could on the thick rugs and quickly fell to sleep in the warmth of the fire.

Before turning into bed, Mak walked over to the long table carved into the back of the cave. He brushed his hand over the long handle of his hammer and smiled, eager to swing it once more. The dwarf was highly skilled with this weapon and it was made entirely out of hardened dwarven rock-iron, including its long handle. Dwarven rock-iron was a metal that appeared as if it had been infused with ultra-hard pieces of jagged rock, which gave it an extremely rough surface that made it difficult to work with. It was difficult to cut and impossible to polish, only the most skilled dwarven blacksmiths were able to work with such a metal effectively and it is the hardest known material in all of Wilstrome. Mak walked over to his bedroll and lay down, keen to get started on their quest.

It was early morning and the rain had stopped, making way for bright morning sun that illuminated the waterfall. Mak was the last one up, having slept off an unknown quantity of strome mead. 'Good morning, friends,' boomed Mak's deep voice, he rubbed his eyes as he rose from his bedroll. 'I see you've found something for breakfast.' Brillo and Tog had found some crusty bread next to the strome mead barrels and had cut it into slices. The others picked some strome berries from bushes they found in the fir tree woods, not far from Mak's cave.

'I hope you don't mind, Mak?' queried Tog.

'No, not at all,' replied Mak. 'It'll only go bad if it's left in my cave whilst we're away.' The bread and berries were placed on the strome mead table with a jug of fresh spring water, and the group stood around chatting and eating their breakfast. New logs had been thrown on the fire to take the chill off the cold morning air.

'Now that our band is complete,' started Plod with a mouthful of crusty bread. 'Let's put together our plan for defeating the beast. We know the sightings have been from its lair in the Loftpeak mountains, so that's where we are headed, does anyone have any experience of this area?'

'Are you not familiar with Loftpeak from the last

time you met, Plod?' asked Mak as he chomped his way through the bread and large red berries.

'Unfortunately not,' replied Plod. 'My party tracked the beast to the eastern mountain ranges and fought the monster just before it descended onto the large mining town of Lodebourne, at the base of the mountains, to wreak havoc.' He looked sad as he recounted these details.

Mak and the others could see that it pained Plod to think about his past experiences with the beast. 'You know, Plod,' said Mak after a few moments of silence. 'Many lives were saved due to the brave actions of you and your band that day. It went into hiding for three years for one and also you prevented the town of Lodebourne from an inevitable attack.' The others nodded in agreement at Mak's words. 'I know many, good, hard working dwarves in the town of Lodebourne, they mine the rock-iron deposits in the eastern mountains. Those good dwarves got to live another day because of your party's courageous action's that fateful day.' He knelt down and put a large, strong hand, much larger than you would expect from one his size, on Plod's shoulder. 'From one warrior to another, you did good that day, friend.'

'Thank you, Mak, your words mean a lot to me,' replied Plod, sincerely.

'Tabs and I have some knowledge of the Loftpeak mountains,' stated Mak. 'We've never been much higher than the base, but I know how to get there and the best route to take us up into the mountains.'

'Excellent,' added Ping. 'But does anyone have any ideas on how we are to defeat the monster?'

'Good question,' said Tam. 'Will our weapons actually be enough to defeat it?'

'Probably not,' replied Mak. 'Let me tell you a short story which, I think may help us in defeating the beast. You may think it's nonsense, but just hear me out.' He had their attention, they leant in, intrigued. 'From a young age there is a short story that all young Wilstrome dwarves will hear, more than once, which supposedly, is true, the tale of the beast blood arrow. The arrow is, as the story goes, a legendary, ancient item, which can, and one day will, defeat the Skinkadink. An arrow tipped with the beast's own blood, the beast blood arrow. During one of the monster's hunting trips in Wilstrome, having descended from its lair high in the Loftpeak mountains, it ravaged a small dwarven village, leaving untold destruction. One brave dwarf challenged the beast. Having nothing else to lose, he managed to slash at the beast when it was upon him, tearing the monsters wing, which is one of the only areas not protected unlike its near-impenetrable, armour-like body. The monster wasn't troubled by this in the slightest and didn't seem to care, its wings were a web of scars from many battles over the years and it would heal. Unfortunately, the dwarf was mortally wounded but his sword was recovered by the village elder shortly after the attack, the blood was still fresh, so he dripped it from the blade into a tankard. The blood was a dark crimson and never dried, it appeared to constantly move and would slither up the side of the tankard as if it were trying to return to its host. Subsequently, the dwarf elder took the blood to another village leader, a hunter adept with bow and arrow. He said if they were to tip the blood somehow in an arrow head, he would use the arrow to defeat the monster. The Skinkadink's blood was concealed within a small glass vial that was set within a recess in an immensely sharp rock-iron arrow tip, which would be capable of penetrating the monster's chest. The vial would shatter, shocking and destroying the creature with energy and power equal to its own, something which, as of yet, the Skinkadink had not experienced, or so the story goes.' His companions' eyes were wide listening to his tale as he looked to each of them in turn as he spoke. 'The only problem with this plan, is obtaining the arrow, it's said to be embedded in the wall, unshattered in the Skinkadink's own lair, after a failed attempt by the hunter to destroy the beast hundreds of years ago. I do believe in this tale, I'm not sure however ... how we go about obtaining the arrow from under its nose. Although if we do, we have the most skilled archer I have ever had the pleasure to fight alongside, in our party.' He turned to Tabs as he spoke, she looked to him and smiled. 'We may have to improvise somewhat, but if we can somehow distract the beast, I would be willing to attempt searching it's lair and recovering the arrow. So, what do you say, guys?'

'Well,' started Plod. 'Although this outlandish story may turn out to be myth, we don't have a better plan and anyway, we're heading to the beast's lair either way, so if we can recover the arrow, then yes, we will definitely attempt to make use of it.'

'I trust Mak's judgement and agree with Plod,' added Tabs. 'If we can recover this legendary arrow from the beasts lair, then I will make use of it when we attempt to kill the monster.'

'Does everyone agree?' asked Plod. 'When we make it to the Skinkadink's lair, we will first try and distract it and retrieve the arrow. Exactly how we go about this feat will have to wait until we have the beast in sight and can work out how best to proceed.' He glanced to his friends as he waited for their answers. It didn't take much thought, whether fact or fiction, they found the dwarf's tale compelling and agreed, if the beast blood arrow exists, they will do everything in their power to use it and destroy the monster in the mountains once and for all.

'When do we leave?' asked Brillo, both anxious and excited to continue their quest.

'Now,' replied Mak. 'If we have all finished breakfast then we have no time to waste. Let's prepare our packs and make a move.' They nodded in agreement and set about preparing their packs for the long journey ahead.

They refilled their water flasks from the stream that ran off the main pool outside Mak's cave and replenished some of their provisions, packing the remaining bread and picking more berries. Tog and Brillo took the crossbows from their packs, which caught Mak's attention, 'Ahh, crossbows, they'll come in handy, lads,' he remarked as he was busy packing his own provisions and a tent in a large leather rucksack.

'They would if we had anymore bolts,' said Tog. 'Brillo commandeered them from the thief-kind, unfortunately we only had one bolt each and they are now in a deceased skimmer on the clifftop.'

'Haha!' boomed Mak. 'Seized them from the thief-kind, great work, Brillo. I can help you with that lad's, one minute.' He went over to a wooden trunk at the end of his bed and rummaged around for a few moments. 'Here, will these do?' Mak dropped twenty or so crossbow bolts on the floor next to Tog and Brillo.

'Great! Thanks, Mak!' said Brillo as they both eagerly grabbed the bolts, taking half each.

'The rift-kin herders gave them to me for free when I was bartering for some of their rift elk meat,' added

Mak. 'Haven't got a clue what they're saying but they're friendly enough folk.'

The others had finished preparing their packs and were ready to leave. Plod had just slid his sword cane into his belt and Tabs secured her bow and quiver on her back, and made sure the belt around her waist, which carried her short sword, was tight. 'OK, are we all ready to leave then?' asked Plod.

They all agreed, except Mak who walking over to his table at the back of the cave. 'Hold on,' he said. 'Just need to grab my trusty old friend here.' He picked up the heavy, gigantic dwarven rock-iron hammer with ease and held the handle near the base, resting it over his shoulder. Mak had a bushy, black beard and only stood 3.5ft tall but had broad, muscular shoulders and a barrel chest, mostly from drinking too much ale over the years. He still had the strength of an ox, maybe even two, warrior dwarves are known for their incredible strength after all. He already looked dressed for battle in fearsome looking jet black, rock-iron plate armour including polished steel gloves, gauntlets and boots. He wore a steel helmet with long back and sides that added extra protection to his face and neck. 'Follow me,' he said as he strode out of his cave and followed the stream into the surrounding wood of tall fir trees.

It was late morning as the group of seven companions walked between the soaring firs, following Mak, north out of Riftbrook. Fortunately, last night's rain storm had passed, and the sky was blue, and the sun was shining brightly. There was still a chill in the air though as the temperature started to drop the further they headed north. 'Mak,' said Ping as they continued their trek. 'How do we exit Riftbrook on this route north? Do we go over the cliffs again and risk the skimmers?'

'A good question, Ping' replied Mak. 'No, don't worry, were not going over the top. The rift-kin tribe who herd the native rift elk have a secure tunnel, they use it primarily for safe passage in and out of Riftbrook to sell their rift elk meat. They don't usually allow anyone else to use it, but I've always got on well with them. Can't actually understand them, but somehow, we always manage to muddle through by gesturing to each other when we barter, they always seem happy to see me anyway. They're solitary, hardy folk, herding the elk in all weathers, no other species has ever managed to control and herd the elk. They are the largest most powerful deer in all of Wilstrome and can easily kill if they charge or rut. The rift-kins though, seem to have an affinity with them.'

'Great,' said Tam. 'I look forward to meeting these interesting folk. What about our journey from Riftbrook to Loftpeak though, Mak? Is that straightforward?'

'Ahh, another good question ... not exactly, Tam,' replied Mak, scrunching his face up slightly, Tabs gave the dwarf a knowing glance. 'We will be travelling through Mammothcap Valley,'

'Oh,' added Plod, now looking quite serious. 'Not straightforward at all then.' The others suddenly looked very interested in learning more about their next destination.

'No, it won't be easy I'm afraid,' said Mak. 'Do you have experience of the mushroom forest, Plod?'

'Only by reputation,' replied Plod. 'I didn't think anyone travelled through Mammothcap?'

'Ordinarily, no,' replied Mak. 'We on the other hand, will have no choice, unless we go around it, possibly adding another couple of days trek to our journey.'

'What, eh ... is so bad about this place?' asked Tog. 'It's a forest of mushrooms, right?'

'It's a wide valley of flat-topped mushrooms,' replied Tabs, 'Not far north from the rift-kins tunnel.'

'It doesn't sound so bad,' said Brillo, looking confused. 'What's the danger?'

'They range in height from a foot,' started Tabs. 'To colossal specimens that can reach over 100ft in height with tops that can sometimes take a couple of minutes to sprint from one side to the other. The danger with going through the mushrooms is the thick, poisonous, soup-like liquid that the mushrooms grow in. Similar to a swamp although highly poisonous to all living creatures, it is thought that this strange liquid is what enables the mushrooms to grow to their colossal size, hence the name, Mammothcap.' Brillo and Tog looked to one another with concern, and the others didn't appear any more pleased with this news.

'If this swamp is so poisonous,' queried Tam. 'How can we pass though it safely?'

'With some difficulty,' started Mak. 'Tabs and I have travelled though this region before. The key to getting through the swamp is more about how you can avoid it altogether.' The others, apart from Tabs, looked confused as he continued. 'We go over the top, literally over the mushroom tops in fact. We use the smaller mushrooms on the outskirts of the valley, where the swamp is at its most shallow and least toxic to jump across the mushrooms and reach the gigantic flat tops above. Even the small ones are extremely strong and will easily take our weight. Once we reach the summit, we can pretty much just walk across them, at this point, the tops near enough meet, creating an overhead carpet of mushrooms across the valley. The important thing is, we stay high and stay away from the poisonous gas produced by the swamp below. It hangs fairly low in the air so we will be fine as long as we stay well above it.'

They continued in silence, contemplating what Mammothcap had in store for them. By early afternoon, the rift-kin tribe could be seen up ahead in a large clearing within the firs, they were herding elk into a spacious pen which was made of thick wooden logs. Even though they farmed the elk, they were respectful and gentle with the impressive animals. None of the animal would go to waist. They provided meat, milk, and leather was made from their hides. The antlers were also used as a crafting material. They were very tall, slender folk and stood at least 8ft high. They wore thick, fur-lined, dark leather clothing made from elk hides, and their long herding canes were crafted from the antlers and were used for hiking as well as herding the elk. Their features were hard to make out as their faces were covered and deeply hidden by baggy hoods, which were sewn into their leather jackets. The rift elk were the largest species of deer in Wilstrome, they were covered in thick, dark red fur and their imposing antlers could grow up to six feet in length. They were strikingly muscular animals, with the adult males weighing as much as two tonnes.

'Here we are,' said Mak. 'The rift-kins are just up ahead, herding the elk,' he nodded in their direction. They stopped when they spotted him and briefly held up their herding canes to welcome him. The rift-kins slowly walked over to greet them. The tallest, in the middle of the welcoming party, leant down and shook Mak's hand. His long, slender fingers easily wrapping around the dwarf's hand. He stopped for a moment, observing the rest of the group and nodded slowly in Tab's direction, having met her before and also shook her hand. Mak motioned to the rest of the group, trying to show the rift-kins that they were his friends. After a few more moments, the tall rift-kin slowly nodded once again and let out a few deep noises that sounded like "whoop, whoop, whoop", he went around the rest of the group, shaking Brillo and Tog by the hand. They had slightly nervous smiles as they greeted the towering rift-kin who was a couple of feet taller than the others. Tam flew over to greet him and excitedly shook his hand with a smile, pleased to meet the rift-kins, he once again let out the whooping noises and seemed happy to welcome the rare, two-footed scritch. He knelt down to welcome Plod and Ping, who were standing on their hind legs as he shook their hands before pushing himself back up on his long herding cane.

'Whoop, Whop,' said the tall rift-kin. They turned and he beckoned the group over, towards the elk pen. 'Whooooop,' said the rift-kin once more whilst waving his cane wildly at the elk. They turned to look at the elk and could see that some of them were rutting and others were kicking their hooves into the dirt or striking the ground with their antlers.

Mak turned from the rift-kins to his own group, looking concerned. 'This isn't right at all,' he said whilst scratching his chin. 'The elk are always so calm in the company of the rift-kins. It's not exactly easy for me to just ask what the problem is, it's difficult enough bartering for elk meat and hides.'

'Let me try,' said Tam as he flew up to the tallest herder and placed a hand on his shoulder. The others looked on with interest.

'Whoop, whoooop, whop,' said the rift-kin, Tam nodded as he spoke and seemed to comprehend everything that he was saying. Tam appeared to communicate with the rift-kin for a few more moments before flying back down to the rest of his group.

They looked at their companion with wide eyes, impressed, eager to see if he had actually learnt anything from the rift-kin. 'It looked as though you understood him,' said Mak. 'Incredible, do you know what the problem is with the elk?'

Tam had a look of unease on his face, 'He blames their behaviour on the monster in the mountains, apparently many animals have been acting out of character recently, such as the cliff skimmers that attacked us yesterday. He thinks the beast is stirring again and the animals can sense it ...' The group looked to one another with anxiously and turned to the rift-kins.

'Whoooooop!' bellowed the tallest herder as he shook his cane frantically in the direction of the Loftpeak mountains.

It didn't take long for Tam to calm the agitated rift-kin leader. Without saying a word, he rested a hand on the tall herder's shoulder and somehow Tam managed to impart the details of the quest they were on and the rift-kin thudded his cane on the floor, excited by the prospect of the beast's destruction. The other rift-kins quickly joined in, creating a chorus of deep whooping noises and the thudding of herding canes.

'Wow,' said Ping. 'I take it they are happy with whatever you have told them, Tam?'

'Yes, very,' replied Tam with a grin. 'They look forward to the imminent destruction of the monster in the mountains.'

'I eh, hope you have mentioned that we are going to give it our best shot,' replied Brillo with a look of concern, not wanting to get their hopes up. 'But success is by no means guaranteed ...'

'Well, I didn't exactly go into the finer details of how uncertain ...' Tam trailed off, mumbling.

'Come on, Brillo,' added Tog, slapping his friend on the back whilst looking equally unsure with an uncertain smile. 'We have to stay positive; we have a plan ... of sorts.'

'Haha!' boomed Mak, grinning from ear to ear. 'That's the spirit, lads, myself and Tabs haven't failed a quest yet, we don't intend this to be our first.' Tabs gave Tog and Brillo a confident smile, but they still looked unconvinced.

'Whooooooop, whop, whop!' shouted the tallest rift-kin, as he started to walk over to the cliffs that bordered their clearing and beckoned them over with his herding cane.

'Come on,' said Plod. 'The rift-kin leader must have

something for us.' The group followed the rift-kin leader together with a few of his tribe, over to their tunnel, which was carved into the cliff. The tunnel is tall and narrow and the leader motions for one of his tribe to enter the tunnel, but he still had to stoop down to make his way through. The party waited for a few minutes, wondering what was going on. The rift-kin emerges with a stack of parchments containing their prized elk meat, wrapped in leaves, he handed them to Mak and slowly nodded to the dwarf.

'Ahh!' said Mak. 'Thank you, my friends,' he grinned, bowing to them in thanks.

The leader slowly strides over to Tam, who fly's up to the rift-kin's head height and rests a hand on his shoulder once more, he nodded as the herder imparts more information to Tam in total silence. 'The tribe leader wants us to have this meat to show their appreciation and thanks for our difficult quest. He has faith that we will be victorious,' said Tam. 'He would also like to offer us safe passage through his tunnel.'

'Ha!' said Mak. 'Excellent news, thank you again, my friends,' he turns to his companions. 'Well, that was easier than me jumping around for a couple of hours, trying to gesture our request, and ending up with a few elk hides.' The others chuckle at this thought.

'Thank you for this,' added Plod. 'We will do everything in our power to defeat the monster in the mountains.' The tall leader stared at Plod for a moment and slowly nodded before bending down once again to shake his hand. He went around the group, seemingly thanking them and shaking their hands before they left for the mushroom forest.

Once the farewells were complete, they shared out

the parchments and stored it safely in their packs. They set off, through the long, narrow tunnel, which had been carved out through the cliff. It was dimly lit, only having a single wall candle every twenty yards or so. It took the band no more than five minutes to exit the tunnel, walking into the shrubland on the other side, headed north to Mammothcap Valley.

The terrain on the other side of the tunnel was rocky with a sparse covering of short grass coating the rocks. Many small, brightly coloured bushes covered in sharp thorns, grew out of cracks in the rock. The odd skeletal looking tree attempted to grow from the difficult terrain, but they were dry and twisted and depleted of leaves. The looming presence of the gigantic mushrooms could just be made out in the distance. A mysterious fog hung over the valley, which was a dark green at the base and gradually rose to a white mist at the height of the largest mushrooms. 'How far do you think we are from the valley?' asked Plod, glancing over to Mak and Tabs as they followed their comrades. 'It doesn't seem too far.'

'No, it's not,' replied Mak. 'At most, it's a couple of hours trek across the shrubland, we'll gradually ascend before we get to a peak that overlooks the valley, then we can walk down to the mushrooms below.'

'Once on the outskirts of Mammothcap,' added Tabs. 'We will need to carefully take a route over the caps and reach the giants at the top. Remember, we need to get way above the toxic swamp below, but fortunately the perimeter won't cause us any problems as the swamp is either extremely shallow or usually dried along the margins.' The others listened with serious expressions as Brillo and Tog shot each other worried looking grimaces.

By early evening, the seven companions came to a halt at the peak, on the edge of the rocky shrubland and viewed the swamp below. They surveyed the giant mushrooms that towered into the sky ahead of them. The sun was starting to set behind the mountains and the valley took on an eerie, dim green haze. 'So, here we are,' said Brillo in a grumpy tone. 'Our next stop, a deadly, mutant swamp of overgrown mushrooms,' Tog chuckled as he gave him a friendly punch in the arm.

'It's starting to get dark,' remarked Ping. 'Are we entering the valley today or camping out and leaving at first light?'

'We don't have any time to waste,' replied Plod. 'Let's press on.'

'I agree,' added Mak. 'We'll make our way up to the giant caps and make a good start. I have a tent in my pack so we can setup camp when visibility is too low. We'll need the cover as the temperature will plummet when it's dark.' Mak led the group onwards and commenced the walk down the rocky hill that became softer the closer they got to the mushrooms. The spongy earth had a slight green tint to it due to the toxins from the poisonous swamp.

'Tam,' said Tabs as they were standing a few feet from the smaller mushrooms on the outskirts of Mammothcap. 'Could you follow these smaller mushrooms up and find the safest and quickest route to the top?'

'Certainly,' replied Tam. 'Give me a few minutes and I'll scout out a route.' Five minutes later, Tam returned with a smile on his face. 'OK, follow me.'

'Great work, Tam!' said Mak. 'Is everyone ready? Watch your footing, the further we go, the more toxic the swamp will be below. I wouldn't fancy your chances if you slip and find yourself in the deadly ooze.' The others watched Tabs and Mak with trepidation as they took their first steps on the smaller mushrooms, no more than a foot high and began their climb, with Tam hovering just in front. Mak went first with Tabs close behind, tentatively following his steps.

Tabs turned to the others, looking stable on one of the small flat tops, 'Come on guys,' she said. 'Just follow our steps, the small ones are much more solid than they look.'

Plod jumped onto the first mushroom top which was still big enough to take him on all fours. 'Let's keep up the pace, guys,' he said to the others behind him. 'We don't want to be jumping across these mushrooms in the dark.'

Ping went next with Brillo and Tog following close behind with renewed enthusiasm. Plod's comments motivated them, and they felt more capable due to their recent climbing experience, scaling the cliffs of Riftbrook. The white mushroom stems grew mostly at crooked angles; the gills on the underside were a dark brown and the caps varied wildly in colour and pattern. Some had black dots or rings covering a white top and others were shades of white, orange, green or blue. As it began to get dark, some of them started to glow in luminescent greens and blues. Tam took the lead, flying up front, as the others followed Tabs and Mak. The glowing mushrooms helped aid them as they scaled Mammothcap. They continued on, jumping from one flat top to another and sometimes pulling themselves up by securing a handhold, digging their hands and paws into the tough, rubbery caps. After an hour or so they had reached one of the gigantic caps at the summit. They all took a moment to sit down and catch their breath after the exertion of the climb, except Tam who only had to deal with a gentle flight to the top. 'Well done, guys,' said Tam. 'How much further shall we go tonight? It's very dark now, other than the faint glow coming off some of the mushroom caps and the light of the moon.'

'Let's set up my tent on that large, glowing, blue flat top over there,' replied Mak, motioning to a huge mushroom cap with a light blue luminescent glow. 'May as well make use of the light, it'll help when we setup camp. I'll light a candle lantern as well.' He rummaged around in his pack for a moment and took out a lantern. He lit it with a small strip of cloth, which he had set alight first with a couple of flints.

'Sounds good to me,' agreed Plod. 'Lead the way.' The others agreed and followed Mak towards the giant, glowing, blue mushroom cap. The dwarf was a barely visible silhouette up ahead, only dimly lit by his candle lantern.

'Whooaa!' screeched Tog as he waved his hands about in front of his face.

'What's wrong?' asked Brillo, who was walking next to him. 'Whooaa! What is that, Tog?' He also waved his hands about frantically as something shot past his eyeline.

'What are you two doing?' inquired Ping. As she spoke, she saw something in the gloom fly past them at speed, she tried to focus her eyes in the dark to make out what it was. 'Hey, guy! Hold up! I don't think we're alone up here!'

Mak and Tabs suddenly came to a stop up ahead and spun around, they walked over to them and Mak held up his lantern, looking around suspiciously. The whole party was now standing together, Tabs gave Mak a concerned look as dark shapes could be seen flying past in the candlelight.

'Not more Skimmers?' asked Tam.

'I thought they flew close to the cliffs?' said Brillo, ducking down slightly as he spoke in a distressed voice.

'They do lad, they do,' replied Mak, turning in all directions as he answered Brillo, using his lantern to try and get a better look at their unwelcome visitors. 'Well, the good news is, they won't be skimmers, the bad news is, I imagine they're cap wings, nothing else lives in the valley.'

'Cap wings, I thought they were a myth?' queried Plod. 'I didn't think anything was able to survive out here, don't birds instinctively avoid flying through or over the valley?'

'Folk think they are just a myth as very few dare to travel through this place,' started Tabs. 'Mak and I have had to venture over the caps on previous adventures, we crossed their path once before.' She was now kneeling, along with the rest of the group as she spoke, watching out for their intruders. 'The only creature that you can see out in Mammothcap are the deranged, cap wing crows. They are native to Mammothcap and it's thought they were once normal, healthy crows but many years ago a small flock made the grave mistake of flying through the giant mushroom forest. Their biggest mistake was weaving through the mushrooms at a low height, inhaling the toxic fumes which hang in the air above the poisonous swamp. They became delirious, insane even and were never the same again.' Brillo and Tog looked to each other with concern, narrowing their eyes as they looked above them. The rest of the group also nervously watched the sky, trying to spot the cap wings. 'Their eyes turned white, and their feathers became tattered and ragged, they never go beyond the outskirts of Mammothcap and usually stay deep within the valley, seemingly slaves to the noxious gas. No other birds or creatures of any sort will enter Mammothcap as they instinctively fear the toxic fumes from the swamp, but the original flock managed to survive and are now a subspecies of crow. No one knows how many live out here.'

'Great,' said Ping. 'More crazed birds to deal with, what shall we do? How dangerous are these things?'

'Now they know we're here,' replied Mak. 'They'll persist in flying past us, until they decide to start dive-bombing, cutting and scratching us with their jagged beaks and claws. They don't like fire though. Last time we had to deal with them, Tabs shot fire arrows at them whilst I attempted to strike them with my hammer as they swooped low, eventually we scared the flock off, and they left us alone. There does appear to be a lot of them though, a lot more than last time ...'

'Fire arrows?' said Tog. 'Out here, what with?'

'The glowing caps, Tog,' answered Tabs. 'They are highly flammable, I just need to cut out chunks of the mushroom and stick the arrow into it, once lit it cracks and sparkles, spitting out flames.'

'Really?' said Brillo, excitedly, wanting to try this out for himself.

'We have our crossbows?' added Tog who also seemed eager to try out the sparkling fire arrows, he grinned in Brillo's direction. 'What are we waiting for?' Their eager grins were short lived, at that moment a few of the circling cap wings dived towards the band, hurtling towards them with their claws facing forward, ready to slash and gouge their prey.

'Lookout!' shouted Plod as he motioned for the party to drop down low. As the rest of the group threw themselves on their stomachs to try and avoid the incoming attack, Plod slid his cane from its sheath at a bewildering speed, jumping to meet the approaching cap wings, he sliced through two out of the three incoming birds in a powerful back-handed arc, cleaving them in two, they bounced lifelessly across the mushroom top and fell over the side. The remaining bird was startled by Plod's response and missed its mark, spiralling back into the air to re-join the circling flock overhead.

The rest of the group quickly got back up, keeping low. 'Haha!' bellowed the dwarf. 'I was looking forward to seeing you swing that cane of yours, weasel, and I was not disappointed, Haha! You've still got the knack then, aye, Plod!'

'The old cane comes in handy from time-to-time,' said Plod as he gave him a sly grin.

'We need to get to that blue, glowing cap!' shouted Tabs over the now angered, cawing birds' overhead, she had her bow at the ready with an arrow pulled back slightly on the string.

'Ready your crossbows, lads!' shouted Mak. 'Follow me! Spread out and stay as low as you can.' They stooped low as they walked at a fast pace in a triangle formation, watching the sky.

There was a gap of about two foot between the flat top they were currently walking across and the glowing blue cap that they were headed towards. 'Watch your footing!' shouted Tabs, before someone fell down the gap between the two mushrooms. They made the short jump and headed to the safer area at the centre of the flat top before coming to a stop.

'You three get your bows at the ready!' shouted Ping. 'I'll get you the chunks of mushroom!' Plod used his sword cane and helped cut out chunks along with Tam who flew over to help and dug into the luminescent cap with his claw-like hands.

Mak stood back-to-back in a circle with the three archers, ready to swing his massive rock-iron hammer in the direction of any incoming cap wings. Once Ping, Tam and Plod had gouged and cut chunks of the glowing cap they ran over to their friends, keeping low. 'Here!' shouted Plod as they approached. 'Let's send these cap wings back to the swamp!'

They took it in turns to spike their arrows into the mushroom chunks, Tabs went first whilst Brillo and Tog kept guard. 'Here,' said Mak. 'Use my lantern candle to light it!' He removed the glass cover from the lantern and Tabs held the arrow over the flame for a couple of seconds, the highly flammable substance lit with ease and she went back to her position. Brillo and Tog did the same in turn and raised their crossbows to the sky, in the direction of the manic cap wings overhead. The chunks let off little sparks of blue flame as they crackled and popped. 'OK, Lads, let's see what you've got!'

The circling flock quickly bolted towards the flat top, moving as one to attack the companions below. Plod and Mak had their weapons at the ready as Ping and Tam held back, they would attack if the cap wings broke through the arrows.

'Fire!' shouted Tabs. She fired her arrow first and it struck the centre of the flock, sending a cap wing into a burst of blue and red flame, which struck the other birds, injuring them. Brillo and Tog gave one another a serious look and nodded, they turned back to the incoming attack and fired their sparkling fire bolts. They both struck the birds with surprising accuracy, sending two of them spiralling over the edge of the flat top in a ball of flames. The flock had now split up, some of them had retreated but others let out high-pitched, angered, cawing sounds. They circled back around and advanced towards them once more. This time they were spread out, hurtling straight for them from all angles. 'Reload and fire as fast as you can!' shouted Tabs. 'Don't stop!' The archers frantically lit more fire arrows and shot them off, taking out more cap wings in bursts of flame as they found their mark. They couldn't reload quick enough as the remaining birds in the flock continued diving towards them, the others would need to hold them off.

'Get ready!' shouted Plod, holding his sword with both paws whilst standing on his hind legs, the blade angled towards the sky. Mak and the others readied themselves. Tam attacked first, he shot forward to meet his foe in the sky, picking off one of the birds, he flapped his wings with immense force at the cap wing, knocking it off course, dazed and confused. He struck the bird with his webbed feet, which caused it to plunge over the edge of the mushroom and tumble into the swamp below.

Plod and Mak swung their weapons with force, slicing and pulverising their targets, the impact of Mak's strike sent one of the cap wings hurtling out into the distance and out of view. Plod turned to him briefly and raised his eyebrows, smiling. 'Haha!' shouted Mak. 'My old hammer also has its uses, Haha!' As Mak spoke, he was unaware of one of the birds coming straight for him. Ping jumped over his head and struck the creature with her sharp claws before it could make contact, lacerating the cap wing. It half flew and half staggered across the surface of the mushroom and plunged into the toxic ooze below. 'Whooaa!' shouted Mak as he ducked. 'Ha! I owe you one Ping!'

The archers let off another round of arrows, which sent more skimmers tumbling into the swamp in a ball of flames. The remaining cap wings circled back around, manically cawing and retreated, knowing they were beaten. 'Yes! Whoo-hoo!' shouted Brillo, jumping up and down with Tog and punching the air in triumph. 'We did it!'

'Well done everyone,' said Plod as he slid his sword back into its sheath. 'We better put your tent up, Mak, it's starting to get pretty cold up here.'

'Right you are, Plod,' replied Mak. 'We'll setup here, on this glowing blue cap, the extra light will come in handy.' The others agreed and set about aiding the dwarf in erecting his tent. Mak set down his lantern on the luminescent mushroom and pulled the tent out of his rucksack. Brillo and Tog decocked their crossbows and placed them safely back into their packs, whilst Tabs put her bow and quiver down beside her comrades' pile of provisions. It was now pitch-black up on the flat tops, other than the eerie glow of their mushroom and the many others that could be seen dotted around in all directions and heights within the mushroom forest. It had taken the companions ten minutes, working together, to setup Mak's old tepee-style tent. The dark green material was fastened to the flat top with ropes, which were secured to the mushroom with some crooked old pegs that had clearly seen a lot of use. Mak slotted together some small wooden poles, these went into the centre of the tent, propping it up. The tent was simple but effective and would keep the band out of the chilly winds atop the giant mushroom. 'OK, guys,' said Mak as he picked up his lantern. 'Here's our home for the night.'

'It would probably be a wise if we keep watch for the night,' said Tabs. 'We'll take it in turns if everyone is agreed?'

'Yes, good idea, Tabs,' agreed Mak, he grabbed his hammer and sat in front of the tent with his lantern. 'I'll go first, I don't imagine the cap wings will trouble us again, but you can never be too sure. I'll wake one of you when I turn in for the night.' Plod and the others agreed with this idea, it was better to be safe than sorry.

'Let's try and get some rest,' added Plod. 'We'll rise early and aim to leave at first light, we don't want to be in the valley for any longer than necessary.' The band of adventurers, minus Mak, who was keeping first watch, crammed into the tent and tried to get some sleep. They used their packs as pillows and were partly laying across each other but it was better than having no shelter at all.

Brillo was the last to keep watch and was sitting outside the tent with his crossbow in hand as his friends gradually rose and stood outside the tent, stretching and yawning. They all helped to pack away the tent and stuff it, along with the wooden poles, back into Mak's rucksack. They had a quick breakfast of the strome berries, which they had collected in Riftbrook the day before and also Mak's remaining crusty bread, which had now gone a bit stale.

The sun crept back up into the sky, ascending from behind the mountains in the distance. They were all packed and ready to set off, Plod slid his sword cane into his belt and Tabs attached her bow and quiver onto her back. Mak grunted as he grabbed his massive hammer and swung it over his shoulder with one hand. They continued, headed over the blanket of huge flat mushroom caps and Tam once again flew ahead and chose the quickest, safest route for their descent. By midday, the companions took their final steps off the mushrooms and left the dangers of Mammothcap Valley behind and headed towards the far greater danger that was their destination, the Skinkadink's lair, high in the Loftpeak mountains.

Chapter 9

Once leaving the mushroom forest, the journey to the base of the Loftpeak mountains was uneventful for the seven comrades. The terrain became increasingly barren and rocky, the shrubs and skeletal trees that they encountered when they left Mammothcap disappeared altogether and made way for a harsh, seemingly lifeless landscape, other than the occasional, well camouflaged, flint horn lizard, that shot past, sprinting over the rocks to find cover in a crack under a boulder. By late afternoon they had completed the trek and were close to the base of Loftpeak, where the next, most difficult leg of their journey would begin.

'Mak,' said Plod. 'How do we get around the creek?' The seven companions were standing beside a deep, freezing creek that ran along the base of the Loftpeak mountains. They stared at the obstacle separating them from the base of Loftpeak for a moment, then craned their necks and took in the imposing sight of the mountain range ahead.

'I'm afraid, Plod,' replied Mak. 'By getting wet … and cold. We can't go around it, the area we're headed is only accessible by crossing the creek.' They shivered at this prospect, other than Tog, who was not troubled much by the cold or freezing water.

As Brillo stared into the freezing, cold water, dreading the swim across, he noticed the top of a mast, sticking out of the water. 'What if we had a boat?' he said, staring at the mast as the water washed over it

'Swimming across and following the base down to Loftpeak's only accessible path is the only way,' replied Tabs. 'If we had a boat, we could just sail down the creek and cut at least a day or more off our journey. We also wouldn't have to contend with the large rock outcrops and the gnarled, twisted trees which grow along the bank, obstructing our way, but we're not that lucky I'm afraid. At around 100ft, this section is the narrowest part of the creek and the safest area to cross.' Mak nodded in agreement at the hunter's words.

'What about that boat,' said Brillo, pointing at the mast sticking out of the creek.

The others looked to each other for a moment, confused. 'Eh, Brillo, it's a nice thought,' said Ping. 'But how would we get it out and how much damage would it have sustained? It has sunk, after all.'

'I would imagine it's also rotten,' added Tam, flying over to his young friend and resting a hand on his shoulder, aware that he was probably thinking about his late father and his own sunken boat, taken into the depths of the River Olden.

'No, I doubt it's rotten,' replied Brillo in a sure voice, still staring at the sunken boat. 'The mast looks in good condition, I don't think it's been here long and the water's pretty clear. From what I can see it doesn't appear to be in too bad shape and the sail is still present. It's a fairly small craft and the water is not too deep, if we could drag it out somehow, I'm sure I could repair it and make it riverworthy again.

'Hmm,' started Plod, not sounding convinced. 'It would be great if we could sail the creek down to the mountain path, but I don't see us getting it out, Brillo.' As Plod was speaking, focused on the sunken vessel along with the rest of the party, Tog rummaged around in his pack for a moment and took out the strong climbing rope, which they had used a couple of days before when scaling the cliff into Riftbrook.

As the rest of the group stared into the creek in silence, Tog shot past and dived into the water with the rope coiled around his shoulder. 'Tog!' shouted Brillo as they went close to the edge of the creek and bent over, searching the water. The faint outline of their companion could be seen quickly approaching the sunken vessel.

'I think he's going to try and secure the climbing rope to the hull somehow,' observed Plod as he stooped close to the water and squinted, trying to make out what Tog was doing.

Tog swam around the boat and cleared a few of the smaller rocks and sunken logs out of the way of the hull and wrapped the rope around the wooden boat's keel, a section of the hull that protruded downward like a fin, strengthening and stabilising the craft. He held on to the other end of the rope and gave a few powerful kicks before reaching the surface and jumped out of the water, landing next to his friends. 'Can't hurt trying to pull it out, can it?' said Tog, winking at Brillo. 'I've removed any obstructions from around the hull and the creek bed tapers out of the water up to the bank like a ramp. It must have been launched here recently. A crack, around a foot in length runs along the bottom of the hull, it was partly resting on a jagged rock on the creek bed, which I've managed to push out of the way. Whoever launched it was unlucky, they would have never got the chance to sail it, I reckon it managed a few yards before it sunk.'

'What do you think, guys?' added Brillo with a grin.

'Well done Tog,' said Plod, smiling at the two friends. 'Perhaps we can give this a go, it will still be heavy though, what do you think, Mak?'

'Haha!' bellowed the dwarf. 'I've been known to drag boulders taller than myself over 100 yards! Pass me that rope, Tog, lad!'

Tabs started chuckling at Mak's sudden enthusiasm, 'OK, let's give this a go,' she said. 'Even if we do manage to get it out, we don't have much time to spend on the repair, will that be OK, Brillo?'

'Yes,' replied Brillo, confidently. 'Let's get it out and I'll assess the damage to the hull.'

Mak took the rope and got himself into position, stomping on the ground a few times as he made sure his footing was solid and warmed up his hands by rubbing them together for a few seconds. 'Watch this!' shouted Mak. 'Ahhhhrgh!' roared Mak as he pulled on the rope, the boat had settled at an angle and wasn't in line with the bank. The others looked on with surprise as the boat began to turn, not expecting the dwarf to make it budge, the stern was now in line with the bank and it slowly started to move towards them.

Plod ran over to help, 'Come on!' he shouted. 'Everyone on the rope!' They all grabbed onto the rope and helped Mak heave the boat up the creek bed.

'It's nearly free!' shouted Ping. 'I can't believe it, its nearly there!' They continued pulling on the rope until the boat was on the bank and clear of the creek. It was on its side, resting at an angle and water was draining out of the boat from the crack in its hull.

'Yes!' shouted Brillo as he jumped around in joy with Tog. The others laughed as they watched their two companions celebrate.

'Ha!' said Mak. 'Well done everyone, well done,' he panted, bending over and resting his hands on his knees. 'I still think I could have got it out on my own though.'

'Of course, Mak,' said Tabs, grinning as she gave Mak a friendly slap on the back as he wheezed. 'We just thought it would speed the process up slightly if we helped.' She winked to the rest of her friends.

'What do you think, Brillo?' said Tam. 'Do you think you can repair it?' Brillo was now inspecting the damage as the last of the water trickled out of the hull.

It was a basic wooden sailing boat, 20ft in length and had no cabin or storage. It consisted of a hull with a few wood boards screwed across its width to act as seating and a simple mast and sail towards the front of the boat. 'Yes, I can repair this,' replied Brillo in a confident tone. The rest of his companions had now gathered around and were eager to hear his assessment. 'The damage is confined to this crack in the hull, otherwise its riverworthy and fortunately the mast and sail is still in good condition. The sail's a bit tatty but it will do us.' He pointed to the damage as he spoke and rubbed his chin, considering the best way to go about repairing the craft.

'You really think you can repair it, Brillo?' asked Tabs. 'We can't spend too long on this; do you think you're able to repair it within a few hours? It will also be dark by then; will we have to wait till first light to set off?'

'Hmm,' replied Brillo, thinking. 'I'll have it ready in two and we'll set off tonight, I'll mount Mak's lantern on the bow and we'll sail through the night,' he grinned, confident with his plan.

The others looked at each other with surprise, they weren't sure if the repair would even be possible with such limited equipment at hand, although, they were excited at the thought of having a working sail boat within the next couple of hours to take them down the creek. 'Ha!' boomed Mak, slapping Brillo on the back and nearly sending him tumbling into the boat. 'That's the spirit, lad! Let's leave him to work, if we can help in anyway, just let us know.'

The rest of the group set down their packs and made a small fire with some of the skeletal trees that lined the bank of the creek. They were now far north, and it was frosty in the day and freezing cold at night. The fire would provide some much-needed warmth and give Brillo extra light to work. The sun had nearly set, and the light level was low. Mak had given Brillo the lantern for as long as he needed it and he spent ten minutes or so carefully inspecting both sides of the crack in the hull with the lantern in hand. 'Mak, Ping' said Brillo, calling his friends over.

'Yes, Brillo,' replied Ping as they both came over to Brillo's side, hoping he wasn't going to say that the repair would be impossible.

'Mak, I need a couple of lengths of your tent and Ping, do you have any remaining cress stem in your pack still, from Cresswood?' He seemed self-assured by his abilities and the items he had requested.

'Yes, lad, of course,' agreed Mak. 'Although we may still need the tent, I'll get it out for you, take what you need from the bottom section and try and leave enough for us in case we still have use for it.' Brillo thanked the dwarf as he went over to his rucksack to retrieve the tent for him.

'Yes, yes, I think I have!' replied Ping, excited that she was able to help in some way, but unsure what use Brillo had in mind for the cress stem.

They quickly returned with his required items and he set the tent down next to the boat. He went over to the fire, holding the cress stem, Mak and Ping sat down with the rest of the group and they all watched with interest as their young friend set to work. He took his penknife from his pocket and stuck the lump of cress stem on the blade, holding it above the fire until it started to bubble and melt, taking it off the flame just before it started to drip. He quickly went over to the boat and smeared the cress into the crack and over both sides of the damaged hull. Once this was complete, he cut away a couple of strips from Mak's tent with his knife and laid them over both sides of the hull. The cress seemed to hold the strips of material in place. Whilst this was drying, he made a couple of simple frames from the gnarled branches found on the bank and secured them in place over the crack on both sides. He used nails he had fashioned from the same wood with his penknife and carefully tapped them in place with a rock.

'OK, guys,' said Brillo as he approached his friends by the fire. 'Let's give it an hour and it will be ready to launch, just need to ensure the cress has dried, it doesn't take long.' It had taken him just under an hour to carry out the repair and would take another hour for the cress stem to dry. His companions looked at him with admiration, impressed with the young boy's quick, efficient work.

'Haha!' said Mak, slapping his knee. 'Incredible!

You're a genius, lad!' The others chuckled at Mak's enthusiasm and Brillo started to blush. 'Let's just hope we make it to the mountain path and don't end up in the creek, do you think it will hold, Brillo?'

'Yes, I'm quite sure,' answered Brillo. 'My father taught me these methods, obviously the wood was of better quality and we wouldn't use strips of an old tent, but yes, it should be just as functional.' They laughed at his comments and congratulated him on his work.

'What was the trick with the cress stem?' asked Tabs. The others also seemed eager to hear Brillo's answer.

'Once melted to just the right temperature,' started Brillo. 'The cress can act as a glue if left to air dry, it also dries extremely quickly and creates a strong, waterproof bond.'

'Wow,' said Ping. 'And there I was, thinking there was nothing new I could learn about cress stem, great work, Brillo.'

'That's good to know, lad' added Mak. 'Let's start getting our packs loaded into the boat so we can launch our new vessel.' The group gathered their packs and weapons together and loaded them into the boat, ready for the launch of the newly repaired craft.

Once their packs were safely on the boat, they waited until the repair was dry enough for the launch. 'What do you think, Brillo?' said Plod. 'Are we ready to launch our new boat?'

'Yes, let's get her in the water,' confirmed Brillo. 'On my say so, we'll push the boat back down the bank. Once it's on the water I'll jump in and throw you the rope. I've already attached one of Tabs climbing ropes to the mooring eye at the bow, pull it tight to the bank and you can all climb in.' They gave enthusiastic nods and smiles and took up their positions behind the boat. 'OK, ready!' he shouted. 'Push!'

They pushed on the rear of the boat and it slid back down the bank into the water. Fortunately, it went in much easier than it came out and Brillo quickly leapt aboard before it floated too far out to make the jump. He didn't have time to wait and see whether it floated or not. His companions on the bank gave cheers as Brillo made the jump. The boat was watertight, and the repair appeared to be holding. 'Haha! Yes, it works!' shrieked Tog with joy, jumping up and down and punching the air. 'Throw us the rope!'

'Catch!' shouted Brillo as he grabbed the mooring rope and chucked it over to his friend. 'It appears I have my first mate back as well!' he said with a pleased grin. The others gave Tog friendly punches as he blushed. He heaved the boat along the bank and pulled it tight into a section that was deep, so it didn't bottom out and then tied the rope to a skeletal looking tree. 'Perfect, thanks, Tog. OK, all aboard!'

Tam flew into the boat and then the others climbed in, carefully taking a seat on the wooden boards nailed across the width of the boat. 'Excellent job,' said Plod, looking around and inspecting their new craft. 'No leaks at all, your father taught you well.' The others agreed and were equally astonished with their young comrade's work.

It was now late evening and very dark, the only light came from the moon and Mak's candle lantern, which Brillo carefully positioned on the bow. Brillo raised the sail and slowly navigated the boat down the creek, coming out of the narrow section and into a much wider part of the creek. The wind picked up and they made good time. He kept fairly close to the bank on the mountain side just in case the repair didn't hold, and they needed to bail. 'It's starting to spit with rain and it's getting cold out here now,' observed Brillo. 'Mak, why don't we use your tent as a cover, place it over the boat, above the boards and you can all try to get some sleep. Just lie down below on the hull, at least it will help keep the wind and rain off.'

'Excellent idea, lad,' replied the dwarf. 'Are you sure though? I'll feel bad trying to rest when you're up here sailing all night in the wind and rain.'

'Yes, I enjoy being out on the water when it's dark,' replied Brillo. 'I used to go out sometimes in the dead of night when I was younger with my father, with just a single lantern, much like tonight. It was peaceful on the river at night, and it felt like a great adventure ... I suppose this is the real deal now.' He smiled to himself, recalling memories of his late-night adventures with his father. He looked up into the night sky, which was a patchwork of densely packed stars and wondered if his mother and father were looking down on him now. The others could see he was lost in his thoughts and didn't want to trouble him. Tog silently sat by his side as they sailed across the creek into the dead of night. The others made use of Mak's tent as Brillo had advised and stretched it across the top of the boat, securing it in place with the guide ropes, creating a simple shelter for the night. They each took it in turns throughout the night to sit with Brillo and keep watch, as he sailed in silence for the entire journey and seemed to have a contented smile on his face, remembering past adventures with his father.

∞∞∞∞

It was very early in the morning and the sun had just started to peak above the mountains, light was still low, and visibility was made worse by the low-lying fog which drifted over the creek. Plod was now sitting next to Brillo as the others tried to get some rest under the makeshift shelter. 'I wonder how close we are to the mountain path,' said Plod, squinting through the fog. 'It's difficult to make anything out in these conditions.'

'I can just about make out the bank in the distance,' replied Brillo, also squinting as he tried to stare through the morning fog. 'I wonder if Mak knows how much further we need to go?'

'Not much further, lad!' boomed the dwarf in the stillness and silence of the creek, startling Plod and Brillo and waking everyone up. 'You've done a great job, well done,' he said as he patted him on the back. 'Just take us towards the bank, I know we're close as I can hear the water splashing in the little bay in front of the mountain path.'

Visibility was difficult as Brillo pushed on the sail boom and headed towards the small bay, through the fog. He then lowered the sail and the boat slowed down and drifted towards their landing area. The bay was a rocky beach set in a little mountain cove, a narrow path could be seen at the back of the cove, snaking up, steeply into the mountain. The path was bordered on one side by a steep mountain, and tall rock outcrops on the other. Gaps in the rock formations led to sheer drops over the edge. It appeared as though it had never been used, as crooked, dead looking trees somehow grew out of the rock and partly obstructed the path. This was clearly an extremely remote and isolated place. Brillo beached their craft on the small rocks without damaging it, which allowed the companions to easily jump off the front of the boat and onto the beach without having to wade through the freezing cold water. 'OK, everyone onto the beach,' said Brillo. He stood to the side as the others grabbed their packs and weapons and disembarked the small sailing boat, leaving Mak's tent in place, covering the rear half of the boat. Brillo was the last to leave their craft, he jumped onto the rocky beach with the mooring rope in hand and tied it securely to a large, jagged rock, which resembled a horn bursting out of the beach. It somehow gave the cove an even more ominous feel.

'You must be tired, Brillo,' said Plod as he looked up at the Loftpeak mountains, piercing the grey clouds high above them.

'Actually, I don't feel too bad,' replied Brillo. 'I enjoyed the journey down here. If I'm on the river, piloting a boat, I'm happy.' The others smiled in his direction as they sorted through their packs.

'Well, you did a great job on the repair,' said Plod. 'I think the boat will take us back across the creek without any problems, there wasn't a drop of water coming through that crack. First, we just have the small issue of the Skinkadink to deal with ...' They all shot him wry smiles, knowing there was a strong chance that they would not make it back down to the cove.

'Before we get underway with our trek up Loftpeak,' started Mak. 'We'll have a good feed, you've been up for hours, Brillo, let's make a fire and cook this rift elk meat.'

Brillo had forgotten about the meat, gifted to them by the rift-kin tribe and his eyes lit up at the thought of cooked rift elk meat. Mak got all the parchments of meat together and stripped the bark of a long stick and sharpened it with a knife from a small belt on his waist. He used some other pieces of washed-up wood to create a spit and sat the large skewer of meat over the top. The others gathered up dry drift wood, which laid scattered about the foot of the mountains, at the back of the cove and dropped it by the makeshift spit. Plod and Mak built the fire, and the weasel took the duty of lighting it, with the flints from his pack.

The creek begun to clear as the fog disappeared and the sun tried to pierce the gloomy clouds encircling the mountains, but it was still extremely cold. The air was always bitterly cold this far north and a crisp breeze came off the large creek, adding an extra chill in the air. Mak slowly turned the meat for thirty minutes and it was ready, the juices from the red meat began to drip and sizzle into the red-hot embers below. They sat around the fire on the rocky beach as the inviting scent of cooked meat hung in the air. They all took a slice and ate their breakfast in silence. The remaining strome berries were shared out and they had a drink from their water flasks. All the food provisions packed for the journey had now been consumed. With breakfast concluded they were ready to begin the final and most perilous leg of their quest. 'Wow, that was good, Mak,' remarked Tog. 'Really good.' He patted his stomach with a contented grin on his face.

The others agreed with Tog's assessment and slowly got to their feet. 'We should pack up and set off,' stated Tabs as she checked the string on her bow and inspected some of her arrow feathers.

They all agreed and made sure their packs were complete before securing them onto their backs. 'I'm going to quickly go on ahead and check out the path,' said Tam as he flew towards the narrow, craggy path at the back of the cove. As he approached the path, a head-splitting roar could be heard from high up in the mountains. It wasn't a deep sound, but a high-pitched, piercing noise, which you could feel in the pit of your stomach and rattled through your head. 'Ahhhhrgh!' shrieked Tam. 'What's that!' He quickly circled back around, away from the path and headed back to his friends who were standing beside the fire.

The others instinctively ducked down and let out startled shrieks at the hideous sound as they looked up at the mountains. All except Plod, who stood up on his hind legs and stared into the cloudy peaks, narrowing his eyes, seemingly unfazed. He had just slid his sword cane into the leather belt over his back and held onto the hilt for a moment longer as he searched the mountains. Mak leapt to his feet and swung his giant hammer over his shoulder, he glanced at Plod and grinned. 'Haha! That sounds like our little friend, Plod!' bellowed the dwarf. He appeared far more jubilant than the rest of his comrades.

'Yes,' replied Plod, shooting Mak a crooked smile. 'It's probably just made a kill; I remember when you could hear its triumphant wails deep into Wilstrome. It sounds like it's getting stronger and more confident,' he added as he stared back up at the mountains.

Brillo and Tog glanced at one another, looking unsettled by the shrill noise. 'Tam,' said Tabs. 'Maybe it's best if we all set off as one and stick together.'

'Ha! Good idea,' replied Tam with a nervous chuckle.

'I imagine the monster in the mountains isn't the only danger that lurks here,' added Ping. She gave Tam a friendly smile. 'Let's all move as one.' With that agreed, they set off and headed over to the ancient mountain path. They formed a tight group with Mak and Plod up front, whilst Tabs hung back at the rear with her bow in hand and an arrow on the string, ready for any unwanted visitors.

They carefully followed the steep path as it arced around the side of the mountain, taking care to avoid jagged rocks and thin trees growing over the trail. By midday they had reached a point where the path took a sharp turn, into the mountain. The steep elevation had flattened out to a gentler slope and the long path widened out to around 30ft with sheer rock formations on either side. They had been walking side-by-side though this wider section of path, but they would soon need to walk in single file again. One of the rock walls ahead of them had a sawtooth-like ridge that gradually tapered down and met a large boulder of rock at the bottom. This was around a foot from the taller, sheer rock wall on the other side, which created a narrow gap for the companions to walk through.

'The path narrows ahead,' stated Mak. 'Single file, guys.' He looked at the tapering sawtooth ridge with suspicion. 'This would be a great spot for bandits, or anything else that wanted to ambush unsuspecting travellers.'

The others now eyed the ridge above them and the

little gap ahead with apprehensive glances. 'Mak, Tabs, have either of you been this far before,' asked Plod.

'No.' replied Tabs. 'We've spotted the cove and path before, from the other side of the creek on clear days, so we knew the old trail was here, but we've never set foot on this path before.'

'No,' added Mak. 'I don't know anyone who has taken this trail, in fact I don't know of any, man, animal or dwarf who has explored this range. I imagine no one has had the chance to recount their tale ... yet,' he grinned.

'Shhhh!' hissed Brillo. He suddenly stopped and put up his hand, indicating to his friends to stop and listen. They spun around to face him, and all froze, listening carefully.

'I hear it!' whispered Ping.

'What is that!' added Tog, as he began to feel a sense of dread building in the pit of his stomach.

A tapping, scuttling sound could be heard from the ridge of the sawtooth rock outcrop beside them. Whatever it was, didn't sound alone. The sound up on the ridge suddenly stopped. They could also make out very slow, cautious tapping near the gap in the path, a few yards ahead of them, coming from behind the boulder. Thin, brown legs slowly appeared, wrapping around the boulder. They were at least two feet long and a few inches thick and covered in thousands of inch long, sharp looking, black hairs. The legs had a crooked appearance due to their many joints. More of the legs began to appear on the boulder and then something crawled into view, framed in the gap between the boulder and the rock wall.

'Rock crawlers!' Shouted Plod, no longer concerned about retaining the group's silence. He slid the sword from his back and slotted the blade's sheath in his belt.

He stood on his hind legs and swooshed the blade from side to side, eyeing the creature in the gap, preparing himself for battle.

For a moment, Brillo and Tog held each other's stare, locked in fear, with eyes wide. 'Haha!' screamed the dwarf, eager to swing his hammer. He gripped it with both hands and held it out to his side. 'Crossbows, lads!' This snapped Brillo and Tog out of their fear as they threw down their packs and retrieved their bows, quickly cocking them and loading a bolt.

Tabs aimed towards the ridge, 'Not long now!' she shouted. 'They're on the ridge as well! It's been a long time since we fought these predators, aye, Mak!' She grinned at her old friend and the weasel as she went back-to-back with them, keeping her arrow trained on the ridge, Brillo and Tog copied the hunter.

Eight long legs met a black, bulbous, oval body, which was covered in jagged red markings. Two long, sharp fangs protruded from its small head, framing two, small, black, dead eyes. It appeared to frantically strike the fangs together, which caused an unsettling clicking noise.

Ping and Tam stood beside one another. 'Ready, old friend,' said Ping with her usual warm smile.

'Always,' replied Tam in a confident tone, returning the smile. He flew above them, to the height of the ridge, his friends briefly looked up to him, catching his gaze. Plod gave him a wry smile and nodded, he turned back to face the predator in front of him. 'Ahhhhrgh!' screamed Tam, in his high-pitched voice. He flapped his wings hard and shot towards the ridge, the spiders started to crawl at speed over the edge of the rock. He smashed his webbed feet into one of them, sending it tumbling down the rock outcrop and smashing into the rocks below in a tangle of twisted legs.

Just as Tam struck the first rock crawler, Plod and Mak rushed forward to engage the ones coming through the gap and over the boulder. They now approached the two comrades at speed, clicking their fangs, eager to catch their prey. Plod jumped over the first crawler and rebounded off the wall next to the boulder, somersaulting on top of the large rock, behind the advancing spiders. As he landed on his hind legs, he thrust the cane into one of the crawlers and kicked it off his sword, sending it down the side of the boulder in a spray of bright green ooze. He dropped down low and swung the sword backward, spinning in a full 360-degree motion, slicing through a number of the crawlers' legs, they stumbled over the rock, slipping in the bright green blood. At the last second, he noticed one was upon him, hungrily clicking its fangs, he dived over it, rolling across the ground and quickly turned, throwing his cane at the incoming crawler, spearing it in the body. It slumped, lifeless onto the rock as he somersaulted back through the air, grabbing his sword cane mid-flight and continued to let off a barrage of intense, dazzling attacks, at a speed which was impossible to follow.

Mak bellowed a deep roar, which for a brief moment, seemed to stop the crawlers in their tracks. He held his giant, rock-iron hammer above his head and swung down hard, crushing the spider that Plod had jumped over completely flat. It sent out a powerful spray of the green ooze, leaving its legs behind intact. Out the corner of his eye, he could see the blur of Plod, spinning, slicing and hacking his way through the oncoming spiders. He had never seen anyone fight with such energy and he grinned at this thought as he continued to smash the huge hammer down onto the crawler heads, making the ground tremble with each strike. They started to instinctively fear the dwarf and reared up on their back legs in a defensive position. He let out an almighty roar, holding his hammer high, they began to back away from him as he confidently approached. The crawlers in Plod's vicinity started to drop back, having witnessed the swift destruction of the weasel's blade.

Tabs let off shot after shot in a blur, not missing her mark, her technique perfect through years of training and natural ability. Her arrows thumped into the bodies of the crawlers with so much force they shot back off the ridge in bursts of green as the arrow heads ripped through them. Brillo and Tog stood next to her and fired off their crossbows. They were much slower but nearly managed to make all of their bolts count. The bolts tore straight through the crawlers and shot out the other side, causing a plume of green ooze to spray from the creatures as they toppled over the ridge.

Ping defended the archers as the spiders were flying off the ridge in a flurry of arrows and bolts. Two of crawlers had crept down the side of the rock face. 'Focus on the ridge!' shouted ping. 'I'll handle them!' The archers nodded and continued their sustained attack, focusing on the ridge above. Ping charged towards the nearest crawler and protracted her claws as she dived at it with lightning speed. It went to rear up and use its fangs in defence but was taken off-guard by the small horn's agility. They tumbled back towards the rock and Ping dug her claws into the body of the crawler as they rolled. She punctured it with force using her horn and jumped free from the creature, as it staggered about and started to shake before slumping lifelessly to the ground. The other crawler turned and tried to make its escape back up the rock face, it was not successful. Ping pounced on it and slashed at its body in a relentless flurry with her razor-sharp claws before jumping to the side, it had already fallen to the floor, motionless, before she landed.

'Ha!' shouted Tabs. 'That's the spirit, Ping!' The crawlers were now in retreat, descending the rocks and finding safety back in their burrows that ran deep into the mountain. Tam continued crashing into them, sending them tumbling down the rocks until they were all out of sight.

The party regrouped. Mak and Plod cleaned off their weapons and they all congratulated each other on a job well done. 'It's an honour to fight by your side, Plod, Haha!' said Mak. 'I've never seen anyone fight like that before.'

Just as Plod was about to return the compliment, a large shadow crept along the rock wall and the light suddenly became dull as if a cloud had drifted in front of the sun. They looked upwards, but it was a sunny, cloudless blue sky. 'Eh, Guys!' said Tog, sounding alarmed as he pointed towards the boulder next to the gap in the path, pulling at Brillo's arm to get his attention. 'What's that coming over the rock!'

The others turned to see what had spooked Tog. 'Whooaa!' screamed Brillo, turning to see why Tog was frantically tugging at his arm. 'Massive crawler! Plod! Mak! What do we do!'

A huge female came into view, creeping over the rock. It had come to avenge its young and was sat at an angle, four legs on the rock boulder and the other four splayed out on the rock wall opposite. Its legs were at least 20ft in length and the sharp black hairs like nails, the fangs resembled tusks, and each were as long as Mak. The clicking sound they made was more like the scraping together of two large blades and the sound echoed off the rock walls. It began to hiss, loudly, smashing its long fangs together.

'OK, everyone just calm down!' said Mak in a hushed voice, his trademark confidence diminishing somewhat. 'No sudden movements!'

'What do you think?' said Tabs, she had an arrow on her bow string, aimed at the massive predator.

'It's too big,' hissed Plod, gently removing his cane from its sheath again. 'I don't think your arrows will trouble it.' Mak picked up his hammer and held it to his side. Tog and Brillo only had a couple of bolts left. They each cocked their crossbows and loaded another bolt.

As the large female slowly approached them, its massive frame brushed over the boulder, its long, thick legs tap across the sheer rock face. 'Look!' hissed Tam. 'The rock wall!' They all glanced at the top of the rock face, small stones and pieces of loose rock were crumbling away from the tall outcrop of rock and cracks started to appear. The spider had stopped and seemed to be eyeing up her prey.

'The rock face!' screamed Ping. 'The top of the rock wall is unstable! Archers! Shoot the top of the wall, not the crawler!' They shoot and more cracks started to appear. Tog and Brillo use their final crossbow bolts, but the wall didn't budge. They slowly backed off as the crawler began to frantically smash her fangs together. Tam flew around in a big arc, headed for the back of the rock face. He hit the back of it as hard as he could and pushed with all his might, trying to help topple the outcrop but it still didn't move.

'Ahhhrrggg!' bellowed Mak, he let out his war cry and charged towards the spider with his hammer held high over his right shoulder.

'Mak!' screamed Tabs. 'Noooo!' The spider hesitated slightly at the sound of Mak's roar. As he approached the crawler, he swung with all his might, not at the spider, but at the base of the unstable, cracked rock wall beside it. The crawler visibly trembled and the seven companions felt the ground shake hard with the force of the dwarf's swing. Tam continued to push from the top and the small cracks are met by huge fractures that run up from the base of the rock, where Mak struck his hammer.

'Whooaa!' shouted Mak as he darted back, towards the group. They all instinctively ducked and moved back from the collapsing rock. The loud splintering, crumbling sound of rock could be heard as the rock face gave way. The massive spider reared up on its legs and faced the disintegrating wall. It let out deafening hissing sounds as it clicked its fangs in a manic frenzy. It was helpless as tonnes of rock tumbled onto the gigantic predator, sending up fountains of green ooze and rock dust as the falling rock crushed it to death.

'Haha! that'll do it!' screamed Plod. He nodded to Tam who by this point had spiralled into the air and was performing a victory lap. He patted Mak on the back, 'That old hammer of yours has its uses then, friend,' he said with a grin.

'Ha!' replied the dwarf. 'Well, I had to find some way of competing with you and that darn sword cane of yours, you were making me look bad, Haha!'

'Oh, I think this has done the trick,' replied Plod, smiling, impressed with the warrior dwarf.

Tabs and the others congratulated him, 'Nice work,' said Tabs. 'I didn't think you still had it in you,' she chuckled and gave him a loud slap on the back.

'Right, now that little problem has been dealt with,' added Plod as he stared up towards the mountain peak. 'We need to focus back on the task at hand, we have a monster to take care of...'

Chapter 10

They had to clamber over the rubble to continue on the mountain trail. A grisly mix of bright green crawler blood and broken rock now obstructed the path. Long, broken crawler legs could be seen protruding from the debris. They continued following the trail in the same formation as before, with Plod and Mak leading up front and Tabs guarding the rear. The steep path zigzagged up the mountain through tall fir trees, their trunks crooked and branches bare. They were nothing like the healthy firs that blanketed Riftbrook. It was late afternoon, and their trek was hindered by low visibility and snow that now covered the mountainside. Fortunately, it wasn't too deep, but it slowed their progress.

The same piercing, high-pitched noise caused them all to stop in their tracks. 'Whooaa!' shrieked Tog as he almost fell into the snow, Brillo grabbed onto him and prevented his fall.

'There it is again,' observed Tabs, glancing up at the sickly-looking firs and snow ahead of them.

'It's much louder now,' added Plod. 'I don't think we're far from the beast's lair, it's in a cave somewhere on this peak.' Mak nodded in agreement, scanning the area and tightening his grip on the hammer.

'We should leave the path,' suggested Ping. 'It's hard to make out the trail in this snow anyway and I imagine the trail won't lead us straight to the monster's front door.'

They all agreed and headed off the trail, treading carefully over the rockier terrain, through the sickly firs and in the direction of the disturbing noise. 'Mak,' said Tam, as they trudged through the snow. 'I think we should light your candle lantern; I could fly ahead and see if I can spot the beast's lair.'

'What do you think, Plod?' asked Mak.

'We really should stick close together,' replied Plod, scratching his head in thought. 'But there's no point in us traipsing through the snow in the dark and heading in the wrong direction.'

'I agree,' added Tabs. 'Let's wait here and take a brief rest; Tam can try and get eyes on the monster's lair and report back.'

'Agreed,' said Mak, the others nodded their approval of the plan. Brillo and Tog leant against a tree to catch their breath, feeling weary after the long slog up the winding mountain path.

'Be careful, Tam,' added Ping, trying to smile through a look of concern.

Mak lit the lantern and passed it to Tam. The sun had dropped behind the mountains and it was fairly dark with an eerie glow that shone off the snow, rebounding the faint light from the moon. The group apprehensively watched as their friend disappeared into the distance, between the rocks and trees. The light from the lantern floated out of view.

∞∞∞

Tam cautiously continued his flight into the wilderness of the mountain, his eyes wide, trying not to miss anything and listening intently for the slightest sound. Even though he had an excellent sense of direction and was confident he would find his way back to his waiting friends, he was apprehensive about going much further. It was extremely dark and the candle in Mak's lantern flickered as the cold, northern mountain air found its way into the glass cover. He hadn't spotted the beast or anything that could possibly serve as the monster's lair. He was about to head back to regroup and work out their next plan of action, when he heard an unusual sound that gave him goosebumps and raised the hairs on his neck. He swiftly flew behind a tree to take cover and made sure the lantern was out of view.

'Just keep calm,' he muttered quietly to himself. 'It's probably just a mountain deer, stripping bark from a tree.' The hardy, tough, mountain deer were one of the few animals to be found on the hazardous mountain ranges, encircling Wilstrome. They would usually strip the firs of bark and eat the needles and roots of the trees, but they were seldom seen, the Loftpeak mountain range was an especially dangerous place for the deer to roam. The sound was coming from about fifty yards ahead, behind a huge outcrop of rock, which jutted out from the mountainside. Tam slowly moved towards the ripping, shredding sound, stealthily going from one tree to the other, fully expecting to find a deer, feasting on the bark of a tree, but erred on the side of caution. He flew behind a fir, which was in line with the face of the large rock about ten yards away. He could still hear the ripping, chomping sounds as he drew close to peer around the side of the tree to observe the deer. He sat the lantern down first, behind the large, crooked fir he was hiding behind and crept out from his cover. The glow of the moon hitting the snow would provide enough light for him to confirm the source of the noise. As he crept further out, the face of the rock came into view, except it wasn't a sheer rock face, it was the entrance to a colossal cave. He gulped as he gently batted his wings and flew, silently to the mouth of the cave. He swooped down quietly into the snow, to the side of the cave mouth and very slowly peered around, into the large cavern.

'Errghh!' he whimpered, quickly covering his mouth to stifle the sound as he stood motionless against the rock, just out of sight of the cave entrance. He had found his deer … it was being devoured by the Skinkadink. The sound of Tam's whimper caused the hulking monster to abruptly stop and shoot its head up from its feast; blood dripping from its enormous, curved beak; its eyes and ferocious looking teeth glinting in the light of the moon. Its head could only just be made out in the shadows, the rest of its body hidden in the darkness. Large, glassy, black eyes stared lifelessly towards the mouth of its lair. It glared for a few moments, totally still, before ravenously returning to its kill of large mountain deer.

Tam felt like his heart was about to beat its way out of his chest. He slowly peered once more around the mouth of the cave, he could see the beast, using the long, hooked claws on its wings and feet to tear and shred the animal apart, ripping the meat away with its powerful, tooth-filled beak. He composed himself and flew briskly over to the lantern, grabbing it mid-flight and hurriedly made his way back to the rest of the party.

The other comrades were huddled under a tree, trying to keep warm when they saw Tam's lantern approach. 'It's Tam!' said Brillo, pointing at the floating candle light speeding towards them. 'He's coming in a bit fast, isn't he?'

They all turned to face their friend as he returned. 'Whooaa!' screeched Tam as he misjudged his landing and skidded through the snow face down, he rolled over and blew the snow out of his mouth. 'The beast!' he panted, breathless. 'The monster, I thought it was a deer! A deer eating bark, but then the rock wasn't just a rock! It was its lair!' He quickly spluttered his words, not making much sense.

'Calm down, Tam,' said Ping, smiling at her friend, she went over and tried to comfort him. 'Slowly now, tell us what you have discovered.'

'OK ... OK,' replied Tam, his breathing returning to normal. He was now able to compose himself, 'I've found the Skinkadink, it was in its lair, a large cavern about twenty minutes flight from here.' The others looked to one another with serious expressions and nodded for him to continue. 'Initially I heard a sound, at first, I thought it was a mountain deer, stripping the bark from wood, I did end up finding a deer ... except it was being feasted on by the beast. The sound I heard, was the monster tearing into it, as it ate. I was petrified it had heard me, as I disrupted its feed, but fortunately it went back to its kill.'

'Good work, Tam,' said Plod. 'Very good work indeed. We must form a plan and attack tonight; we can't risk making camp for the night anyway.'

'Yes,' agreed Mak, 'The cover of darkness might aid us as well. So, what do you propose?'

'We split into two groups,' replied Plod. 'One will distract the beast and the other will enter its lair and try to locate the beast blood arrow.'

'OK, Plod,' added Tabs. 'It's the best and only plan we have, so what will the groups be?'

'We need a quick, agile group to get the beasts attention,' replied Plod. 'So definitely Tam and Ping for a start,' he looked to them as he spoke, and they nodded confidently. 'I think I'll join Tam and Ping in drawing the monster away from its lair. The rest of you will assist Mak in searching the cavern for the legendary arrow. Tabs will obviously need to be part of this group as she will be taking the shot. Brillo and Tog are out of bolts now anyway, so it makes sense to have the extra help, searching its lair.' They also nodded their agreement with the plan. 'We just need to work out the best way to distract it.'

'I'll fly into the cavern and lure it out,' started Tam. 'The searching group can wait around the side of the rock and run through the cave mouth as soon as it begins its chase. I'll fly down the mountainside and Plod and Ping can run ahead of it, on either side, it won't be able to stop all three of us at once.'

'Good idea, Tam,' agreed Plod. 'Whatever happens, keep going, like Tam said, it can't stop all three of us at once. As long as its distracted, the searching team can hopefully retrieve the arrow. We'll try and distract it for as long as possible before circling back, towards its lair, where hopefully you'll be waiting to take the shot.'

They all looked to each other with sad smiles, aware that at least some, if not all of them, would likely fail to make it home safely to Wilstrome. 'Don't let it catch you,' said Brillo, looking to Plod, Tam and Ping in turn, his voice breaking as tears formed in his eyes. Tog looked equally upset at this prospect and put his arm around his young friend to comfort him.

'No one is being caught lad!' boomed the dwarf, now standing up with a grin. 'Not if I can help it!' Mak's enthusiasm made everyone chuckle as it took the edge off the serious task ahead of them.

'With the plan agreed,' said Plod. 'We have no time to waste, let's get our packs together and follow Tam to the Skinkadink's lair. This is it, guys, this is what we came here for ...' They set about putting on their packs. Tabs checked her bow string and hoped the plan would work, she was also out of arrows after the rock crawler attack, they only had one chance of success, the beast blood arrow was their only hope.

Tam led up front and Mak held the candle lantern as the searching group would need it to locate the arrow. Tam's keen sense of direction didn't let them down as it wasn't long before the large rock outcrop, containing the beast's lair, came into view up ahead.

'OK,' whispered Tam. 'This is its lair, is everyone ready?' They had silently made their way over to the rock wall and were all pressed against it. The searching group agreed, if somewhat hesitantly. Tog and Brillo

looked to each other and gulped. They composed themselves and shot one another an assured glance, there was
no time to back out now. 'Here I go!' hissed Tam before
flying into the mouth of the cavern. After a few moments,
a blood curdling, high-pitched scream could be heard
echoing out of the cave. The others exchanged worried
looks as Tam still hadn't emerged. A tremendous crashing and the sound of gigantic, powerful wings flapping
could be heard. 'Whooaa!' screamed Tam as he burst out
the cave mouth. The enraged monster sprinted as fast as
it could, hunched over, flapping its enormous wings, in
attempt to get its hulking frame airborne to snare the unwelcome visitor.

Plod and Ping turned to the rest of the group. 'Good
luck!' shouted Plod. 'We're up, Ping, let's go!' They nodded to the rest of their friends, possibly for the last time
and bolted after Tam and the Skinkadink. Ping shot towards one side of the beast and Plod the other, they raced
down the mountainside at dizzying speed. The monster
quickly realised that it had more than one unwelcome
intruder on its mountain and hung back slightly, uncertain if it should attempt to take off and go for the two-
footed scritch, or one of the creatures running alongside
it. It furiously looked from side to side, making ear-split-
ting wailing noises towards Plod and Ping. It jolted to
the side and took a frenzied swipe at Plod with its wing
and then did the same to Ping. Fortunately, they easily
dodged its confused attacks before the monster focused
once more on Tam, who had now dropped back down to
its eyeline to tempt it once more.

'In we go!' hissed Mak, trying not to make too much noise in case he alerted the chasing Skinkadink. He held up his lantern and scanned around as he quickly entered the cave mouth, the others followed closely behind. The remains of the deer were visible in the centre of the large cavern and many other bones and skulls from previous kills were scattered about the cavern floor. Mak set his lantern down in the middle of the cave, which bathed the cavern in a dim glow, but it was enough for them to carry out their search. 'OK, guys, split up,' said Tabs. 'Let's find this arrow!' They spread out across the cave wall and carefully began their search.

Within minutes they had finished searching as much as they could in the dim candle light. 'I can't see it!' hissed Brillo. 'Tog, what about you!'

'Nothing!' replied Tog. 'Tabs! Mak!'

'Let's go again!' replied Tabs.

'It has to be here somewhere!' added Mak. They continued their search, meticulously studying the cavern walls.

The Skinkadink was busy crashing over the mountain-side, in pursuit of the unwelcome visitors. They had now circled back up towards its lair and just hoped that the others had been successful in their search for the arrow. Tam zigzagged in front of the beast and swooped up and down, sometimes darting through the trees and then spiralling into the air to confuse it. 'Haha!' shouted Ping. 'That's it, Tam! It doesn't know whether to run or fly,

Haha!' As Ping was cheering Tam on, the beast suddenly darted to the side and went to swipe a massive wing in Ping's direction, taking her off-guard and very nearly taking her out.

'Be careful, Ping!' shouted Plod, his heart now racing at the sight of his friend's near miss. 'Not long now! Let's hope they have the arrow and are ready for us!'

∞∞∞

The search in the cavern still hadn't produced the beast blood arrow. If the arrow was hidden in the cave, they couldn't find it. 'Ahhhhrgh!' screamed Mak, getting frustrated with the search.

'We haven't got long now!' shouted Tabs, no longer concerned about alerting the Skinkadink to their presence. 'I can hear it coming back up the mountainside!'

'What shall we do now, Mak!' Shouted Brillo, feeling helpless.

Tog was still frantically searching the walls, terrified, muttering to himself as he swept his webbed hands across the wall. 'Ahhhrggh!' he screamed as he tripped over something at the back of the cave. The others ran over to help him up. 'Thank you, I must have tripped over a rock or something.'

The others looked down as he brushed himself off, their eyes widened as they all shouted at the same time, 'The arrow!'.

'Haha!' screamed Mak. 'You found it, Tog!' Brillo smiled at his friend and patted him on the back, they couldn't help but chuckle.

'Quick!' shouted Tabs as she took the bow from her

back. 'We need that arrow now!' Mak yanked the arrow from the wall and nearly fell backwards as it came free; he handed the arrow to the hunter.

At that moment, the Skinkadink slowed as it approached its lair, sensing something was wrong. It was no longer interested with its chase outside and clattered into its cave, letting out a head-splitting, high-pitched roar.

Tam dived back down to Plod and Ping who were a few yards from the mouth of the cave. Plod quickly drew his sword cane and threw the sheath into the snow.

The monster was coming straight for them, shaking its head hysterically and wailing, its beak wide open, showing its terrifying rows of backwards-facing teeth. 'Get out of here, lads!' yelled Mak as he raised his hammer to the side and let out his own war cry. The monster briefly recoiled in surprise and observed the dwarf with suspicion, silently glaring at him with dead eyes. Whilst the beast was focused on Mak, Tog and Brillo sprinted around it and stood by their friends, who were waiting nervously, outside in the snow.

Tabs had the arrow trained on the monster and was waiting for it to lunge towards Mak, wanting a clear shot at its chest. The beast snapped out of its trance and rather than going for the dwarf, it swooped its wing around in a powerful arc, taking Tabs by surprise and struck her hard, sending her smashing into the cave wall. She fell to the ground unconscious.

'Noooo! Tabs!' screamed Mak as he ran towards the monster and struck it in the leg before it had a chance to react. It let off a piercing scream in anger and smashed Mak and his hammer against the wall with its wing. Mak fell to the floor and then staggered to his feet. He went to pick up his hammer, but everything turned black, he passed out from the attack.

The Skinkadink turned, limping on a crooked, broken leg. It was drooling and eager to catch the rest of its prey. The five remaining companions stared back at the monster as it turned and glared at them. 'Mak! Tabs!' shouted Brillo. 'What now, Plod!'

Plod controlled his breathing and returned the monsters glare for a moment, thinking about his next move. The beast cocked its head to one side, remembering this foe from before as it let out a pained roar. He swooshed his cane to the side and shot off at lightning speed, catching the Skinkadink by surprise. He slid under its legs and slashed a gash in its underside; it let out an angered scream. He rolled to the back of the cave and stopped next to Tabs. He picked up the arrow and stroked her head with his paw, hoping they would somehow get out of this alive. 'Tog! Brillo!' shouted Plod. 'One of you must fire the arrow! Get your crossbows!' Tog and Brillo chucked their packs into the snow and quickly pulled out their bows.

As the monster advanced on Plod, Ping ran into the cave. 'Plod!' she screamed. 'Throw me the arrow!' Plod threw the arrow just before the monster smashed him into the cave wall. He landed next to Tabs, motionless. The arrow slid across the floor and Ping grabbed it in her mouth. She ran back towards the cave mouth, quickly turning her head to see a massive wing coming straight for her. She slung the arrow from her mouth, just before the wing struck and everything went black for the brave small horn.

'Noooo! Plod! Ping!' shouted Tog.

'Quick!' shouted Tam. 'The arrow!' He shot towards

the cave mouth and picked up the arrow. He threw it in the direction of Tog and Brillo whilst spiralling into the air, managing to avoid an incoming attack.

The arrow landed closest to Tog. He grabbed it and tried to cock his crossbow and load the arrow. He fumbled anxiously and didn't notice the incoming attack from the monster's wing as it swept towards him. Brillo ducked and avoided the gigantic wing just in time. Tog wasn't so lucky, he was sent flying into a fir tree and crashed with a sickening thud. He fell lifelessly into the snow.

'Tog! Noooo!' screamed Brillo. He dived for the arrow, which was sticking out of the snow. He frantically tried to cock his crossbow and load the arrow. He looked up and the Skinkadink was upon him, merely a few feet away, its massive beak open and roaring in his face, it went to strike him, as it thrust forward with its fearsome teeth.

'Ahhhrrggg!' screamed Tam as he dived towards the monster and batted his wings in its face. The beast was briefly startled and reared back, its wings wide open and its chest in full view. Brillo threw himself backward into the snow and aimed his crossbow. He paused for a moment and composed himself before taking the shot, this was their only chance. The Skinkadink went to lunge forward again. 'Now!' screamed Tam.

'Ahhhrrggg!' screamed Brillo. 'No one hurts my friends!' He pulled the trigger. The bolt shot through the air and shattered the monster's chest. The arrow drove into its heart and the small glass vial containing the Skinkadink's blood exploded, sending out a shockwave of energy that caused its heart to burst. The enormous beast let out a blood curdling scream as it staggered backwards with wings outstretched. Suddenly it went completely silent and still as it crashed onto its back, sending up plumes of snow and lay there with its beak half-open; its eyes staring lifelessly up at the sky. The Skinkadink was dead.

The seven friends remained on the mountainside for another week, using the Skinkadink's lair as shelter. Tam managed to use his healing energy to slowly treat his companion's wounds. Brillo aided him in caring for their wounded friends and one-by-one they came around. It had taken a full week for the five injured comrades to build up enough strength to make the gruelling trek back down the mountain and take their boat, moored in the small mountain cove, back across the creek.

'Are we all ready to leave?' said Plod as he slid his sword cane in place over his back.

'I think so,' replied Tabs. 'I can't believe we did it ... or should I say, Brillo, the expert hunter.' They all grinned at their youngest companion.

'It was a team effort,' replied Brillo, blushing with a half-smile. 'I barely did anything, it was more luck than judgement, I just pulled the trigger.'

'Haha!' bellowed the dwarf, clutching his side and wincing as he laughed, due to painful bruising on his chest that was still healing. 'You're too modest lad! You and Tog were both prepared to die on this mountain to defeat the Skinkadink and save your comrades. I would be honoured to fight by your side again.'

'Let's hope that moment doesn't come too soon,' replied Tog. They all chuckled with the gillsprog.

Ping walked over to Tam and gave him a warm smile, she wanted to thank him for all he had done for her and her friends but couldn't find the right words. 'Tam ...' she said, 'I ... thank you,' She embraced her old friend. The others went over and did the same, struggling to put into words their gratitude and respect for the two-footed scritch who had healed their wounds and saved their lives.

Before they descended the mountain and left the Skinkadink's lair behind, Mak went over to the fallen beast and took out his knife. He extracted seven teeth from the monster's colossal mouth and cleaned them off in the snow. 'Here,' said Mak, handing a large, sharp tooth to each of his companions. 'These teeth will serve as our proof that the Skinkadink has finally been vanquished from Wilstrome. It will also be a reminder of what the simple folk of Wilstrome are capable of.' He looked at them in turn as he spoke with a sense of dignity and pride. 'Do not doubt the importance of what we have achieved, friends, we walked selflessly into oblivion and came out the other side victorious.' They stood in silence in front of the monster's lair for the last time and looked out across the beautiful landscape of Wilstrome. It was finally time to go home.

Chapter 11

Brillo sailed the boat, back across the creek at the base of the Loftpeak mountains. They took a longer route, avoiding the dangers of Mammothcap. Speed was no longer of utmost importance as they headed towards Walnut Point. They had all agreed to stop at the little walnut tree village as a group and tell the old dwarf, Frilldar, of their quest and show him their proof, the Skinkadink's teeth, one for each member of the party.

After a long and tiring journey back into the dense woods, deep into Wilstrome, the seven companions walked into Walnut point with Tam and Plod leading up-front. It was early morning, and the sun was burning off the mist hanging over the village. As they passed Plod and Tam's house, wisps of smoke could be seen on the other side of the village, coming from outside a large walnut tree house. It was Frilldar, leaning against his tree, having a smoke on his pipe as he did every morning.

'Wait a minute,' mumbled Frilldar, squinting through the morning mist. 'Haha!' he bellowed. 'Is that my good friends, Plodweasel and Tamfoot!' He rested his pipe on a cut log next to his tree and approached the group. 'Ha! And you bring friends, I trust you have good news for me?' They all stood on the little stone bridge, over the village brook.

Frilldar's smile started to slip, and a look of worry spread across his face, hoping that the returning heroes had good news. They all held out their hands and slowly opened them, revealing the teeth. 'Indeed Frilldar,' said Plod, now grinning along with the others in his band. 'The hunt was successful, the Skinkadink is dead.'

'Haha! Yes!' shouted the old dwarf, attempting to jump in the air and click his heels in delight. 'I never doubted you, either of you. Now you must introduce me to the rest of your party and tell me the details of your quest.' He eyed each of them carefully and smiled when he recognised a familiar old face. 'Makledar! You old brute! It's been a long time, too long in fact.'

'Ha!' replied Mak. 'It's good to see you again, old friend.' He put his arms around the old dwarf, and they gave each other powerful slaps on the back.

'You're all welcome to stay for as long as you wish,' said Frilldar. 'You can use a couple of the empty homes, next to Plod and Tam's place. I'll make sure the strome mead is flowing later on and you can tell me all about your adventures, Haha!' They all chuckled and Mak had a massive grin on his face, looking forward to a cold tankard of strome mead.

Plod and Tam were happy to be back home, exhausted from the long journey. The others got some much-needed rest in the vacant walnut tree homes. Tog and Brillo shared one and the others made use of the remaining empty house. Later that evening they dined at Frilldar's tree. He had invited leaders of the surrounding towns and villages, who had tasked Plod with putting together a band once more, to defeat the Skinkadink. They spoke late into the night and the leaders hung on their every word, impressed with the seven companions enthralling tale. Plod and Tam's new friends agreed to stay for a few more days, they needed the rest anyway. The journey back from the mountain had been long and tiring and they were still healing from their confrontation with the monster.

The day had arrived for the friends to say their goodbyes. They were all stood outside Plod and Tam's home, including Frilldar. It was mid-morning, the sky was cloudless and blue, and the sun shone brightly, it was a warm, pleasant day. 'You're all welcome to return whenever you wish,' said the old dwarf. 'Where will you go, Tog, now that your homeless? As I've said peviously, you're more than welcome to take up permanent residence, here, in Walnut Point.'

'It's a lovely offer, Frilldar,' replied Tog with a smile. 'I think I need to be back on the river, it's where I belong.' His smile slipped as he became lost in his thoughts, unsure of where he would end up, no longer welcome in his home town of Olden's Moat.

'Oh, you'll still be next to the river,' grinned Brillo.

'What do you mean?' replied Tog, looking confused.

Brillo punched his friend, playfully on the arm, 'You're coming to live with me in Clamshell Nook, in my hut. I could do with a lodger, it's pretty lonely on my own. We'll get a new boat and start a business together, fishing the River Olden. What do you think, fancy being my first mate?' He smiled at Tog, waiting for his response.

'I ... don't know what to say,' replied Tog with tears in his eyes.

'Haha!' bellowed Mak. 'I think that's a yes, young Brillo. You'll make a fine team!' The others agreed and patted Tog on the back, he was overcome with emotion.

'And what about you two,' said Frilldar, motioning to Tabs and Mak.

'I've got something important to show the rift-kin,' grinned Mak, holding up his tooth. 'I think I'm in line for a lifelong supply of rift elk meat.' They laughed as Mak proudly held up his ticket to an unlimited supply of elk meat.

'I must get back to the Guild & Inn,' added Tabs. 'I'll have some tales to tell the other adventurers of the guild. If it weren't for the tooth, I'm not sure how much they would believe. You're all welcome to come and stay at any time, there will always be a warm bed and a tankard of cold strome mead waiting for you.' She smiled as they all agreed to take her up on the offer sometime soon.

'And finally, Ping,' said Frilldar. 'I take it you'll be going back to Cresswood?'

'Yes,' said Ping with her warm, friendly smile. 'The other small horns will be wondering where I disappeared off to in such a hurry. I can't wait to tell them stories of our adventures. I'll be back to visit Walnut Point again soon, small horns rarely leave the hamlet, but I think I've got a taste for exploring Wilstrome, outside of Cresswood.'

They said their final goodbyes and hugged one another, hoping to all meet up again soon, hopefully under more pleasant circumstances than the first time. Plod and Tam stood outside their tree, next to their old friend, Frilldar, and watched as their companions left

Walnut Point. The last person to step into the woods and leave the village, was their friend, Brillo. The young, orphaned boy and proud fisherman's son, from the village of Clamshell Nook, who defeated the monster in the mountains with a single arrow, bursting the Skinkadink's heart.

The End

Acknowledgement

Thanks mum (Denise-Ann). Thank you for taking so much time to read through the book for me :)

About The Author

Bradler Smith

 I started writing short stories based on the rambling conversations I would have with my right-hand man, my little boy, Bradley, but they would always end up longer and too complex for a 3- to 4-year-old to easily understand. I took some of our ideas and decided to write some fantasy fiction - and also, now, some horror ...

Books By This Author

Lombard & Meer: One Hat To Rule Them All!

***A quest fantasy/fantasy fiction adventure ...

Our tale takes place on a planet known as the Bowstar. Four friends embark on a heroic quest to recover an unremarkable looking item, a hat which grants the wearer a single wish.

Meer the meerkat along with his best friend, Lombard, a small plant-eating dinosaur of a nervous disposition, team up with two equally unlikely-looking adventurers. Blur, an old wood elf and his lifelong friend the old monocle wearing flamingo, Twiglet, team up to reclaim the stolen magic hat. The hat in question has been pilfered by a raven known as Jantrix, the right-hand raven of the evil old wizard Sparlax, who resides in his castle situated on the near impenetrable Mount Loon.

The four adventurers have to retrieve the hat before the scheming wizard uses it to rule over the Bowstar. They will visit strange and obscure places and meet a range of characters on their quest, some will aid them and others will hinder their progress.

The fate of the Bowstar and all who live on it will be in their hands!

Beechnest Lane

A horror thriller set down a remote woodland lane. Larry swaps North London for a quiet house in the Chilterns, and possibly, not for the better ...

For the first time in many years, one of the houses down Beechnest Lane has come up for sale. A small, private Lane of Edwardian houses, set within a remote woodland of beech trees. The houses down the lane have been unoccupied for years and now number 12 has been put on the market - for an impossibly low price. It has a history though, and not a pleasant one. Will the unwitting new resident of Beechnest Lane, still be pleased with his purchase once he learns its history, which was left undisclosed by the agent.

The sudden appearance of Larry, the proud new owner of 12 Beechnest, doesn't go unnoticed. His presence has caught the attention of something, or someone, deep into the woods surrounding the lane.

Will history repeat itself, will the first resident of Beechnest Lane in decades ... also disappear?

Printed in Great Britain
by Amazon

86517331R00107